The O'Connell Family Christmas
Paperback Copyright © 2022 Lorhainne Ekelund
Editor: Talia Leduc

ISBN-13: 9781998775224

Give feedback on the book at:
lorhainneeckhart@hotmail.com

Twitter: @LEckhart
Facebook: AuthorLorhainneEckhart

Printed in the U.S.A

The O'Connell Family Christmas

THE O'CONNELLS
BOOK FOURTEEN

LORHAINNE ECKHART

As Christmas approaches, the O'Connell family's loyalty is tested once again.

Owen O'Connell wants only one thing: to put a ring on the finger of his long-time girlfriend, Tessa Brooks. But when her past fears become an obstacle between them, Owen may not get the new beginning and the happily ever after he truly wants.

Meanwhile, Suzanne O'Connell finds herself in a year-long slump, being the live-in girlfriend of Deputy Harold Waters. Jobless and searching for something to give her life meaning, she finds herself on the wrong side of the law when she stands up for the rights of a stranger who is targeted by the community. Suzanne, who is known for her stubbornness and her obstinate sense of right and wrong, ends up taking on a woman no one else will, and in doing so, she tests her relationship not only with Harold but with every one of the O'Connells.

As the O'Connells work together to keep their sister out of jail, can big brother Owen, who has been a father figure to all his siblings, achieve the future he dreams of with the only woman he's ever truly loved?

CHAPTER

One

"I want to get married," Owen said, not pulling his gaze from Tessa, who was holding a chef's knife, chopping peppers on the butcher block island he'd finished installing.

She seemed to freeze, then slowly lifted her eyes to him, still holding a red pepper. Wow, those blue eyes really packed a punch at times. Her frizzled wavy blond hair was in a loose ponytail, and she was wearing one of his T-shirts, the one he'd been looking for, with *Nashville* written across the chest in black.

"And who is it you want to get married to?" she said, lifting a brow and going immediately to teasing, tossing out her edgy, twisty, sarcastic humor. It was her go-to, he had learned well, when she was uncomfortable or when something turned serious.

"…Snow White?" he said. "Seriously, Tessa, you're the only one I'm interested in sleeping with, living with, and being in a relationship with." He slid around and swept his hand across the empty room around them, with only the kitchen table and four chairs. "Come on.

You and me, we should get married. You know there isn't anyone else. I'm being serious, here."

He had to fight the urge to laugh at her expression, because there it was again. Her eyes widened, the blue flickering as if she were about to laugh or change the subject, or maybe she was wishing for an interruption so she wouldn't have to answer him.

"And don't do that, there," he said, gesturing between them. "I can see you're freaking out."

"I'm not freaking out, Owen. That's ridiculous. But, seriously, what's the rush? Things are good. Why do you want to go and wreck something that's working perfectly? This thing between us is good, and now you want to mess it up?"

She gestured with the butcher knife, and he found himself staring at it, the way her hand gripped it. She was getting loud, and he could hear the panic cutting into her voice. He pulled his arms across his chest, leaning back on the bar stool at the island, and then reached out and gripped the hand that held the knife. He pulled it from her, and for just a moment, he wasn't sure she'd let it go.

He said not a word, as she seemed to grip it harder. "Tessa, let go. Seriously, I'd rather not be on the receiving end of this with you holding a knife. Come on." He pulled again, and this time she let go and stepped back, slim, sexy, gorgeous—and his, almost. "You know, getting married isn't a death sentence. You're making it seem as if it's the end of the world when it's not. We've been together a long time. Hell, the rest of my family is getting married around me: Ryan, Marcus, even Brady, who's just a kid marrying a kid."

She let out a rude noise and lifted her hands in the

air. Then, instead of saying anything more, he watched as she walked out of the kitchen. He could hear her in the hall, then in the bedroom.

"Great, just great, O'Connell," he said under his breath, putting the knife on the island.

He stood up and started out of the kitchen, taking in the small artificial Christmas tree plugged in on the sofa table by the living room window. Striding down the hall, he noted that the wall and trim on one side still needed a coat of paint.

In their bedroom, Tessa was in just a pair of pajama shorts, her back to him, pulling on a bra and fastening it. She reached for a black knit, which she pulled on over her head, and pulled her long hair free from the ponytail.

As he stepped up behind her, their eyes connected in the mirror. "I love you. You know that, right? But you didn't answer me on why this is freaking you out so badly. I knew I'd likely have to do some convincing, but I'm starting to get the feeling you're leaning more towards a no, and I can't help wondering if this is about me."

She looked at him as he set his hands on her shoulders, then over her hair, which needed a good brushing. Then she turned around, resting her hands over his chest, looking up at him. He could feel what a perfect fit she was, but he knew there was something there, some unseen obstacle. He wondered whether she even understood why she instinctively pulled back on so many things. The problem was that for him, it hadn't been a big deal until now.

"Why do you need to get married?" she said. "This is perfect. And why are you suddenly comparing us to your brothers? So what if they get married before us? This isn't a race, you know, and marriage is the kind of institution, frankly, that I equate to people suddenly not having to be on their best behavior, breaking promises, and slowly beginning to hate each other. And let's not forget keeping secrets." She gestured toward him, then pressed her hands to his chest again, running them over it, before letting them fall to her sides.

He couldn't get his head around what she'd just said. Hating each other, keeping secrets? He supposed lying was coming next. He realized, as he stared at her and the mixed emotions staring up at him, that she really believed what she'd said.

"Okay, firstly, that's absolutely crazy thinking, Tessa," he said. "You know I don't have any secrets from you. You know every one of my secrets and every dirty, dark, crazy thing that has happened in my family. What this is about is you and me. I can't believe you're automatically taking a twisted view of how things will be. This has me thinking we're talking about your parents, but we're certainly not Jill and Ted Brooks. They chose to live that lie, that life of broken promises and disappointments, being together, laughing one moment but trash-talking each other behind their backs the next. I mean, seriously, Tessa, I'm pretty sure you would never do that to me, and I can tell you, no matter how angry I get with you sometimes, I'd never cut you up like that. What happens here is between you and me. I'm not going to dissect your character behind your back."

She was so close, and for a moment, he thought she was getting it. She was right there, but she didn't touch him, though he could see she wanted to. Maybe it was the way she was fisting her hands, but he could see the tension in her. He could have just pulled her close and ignored this thing she was feeling and freaking out over. She hated the bickering and back and forth between her parents. It was just one of her quirks, just one of those things that made her who she was.

He'd never realized she was convincing herself that could be them. He hadn't seen that coming.

"This is perfect, what we have," he said. "You're right, but I want to get married. I mean, you're it, and marriage is just me saying there's no one else. You know we're together, and marriage is a natural evolution. We found each other. I love you. We get married, become a family, have kids. I seriously see myself growing old with you, and it excites me, knowing you'd be right there in our old age, racing me down some nursing home hall with a walker, with our grown kids visiting, and our grandkids…"

He had to stop talking, though, because she wasn't smiling. In fact, her frown deepened. Apparently, she wasn't holding on to the same dream he was.

"Then comes the disappointment and broken promises," she said.

Oh, there she went, reverting to that lifetime of hurt she seemed to carry, that pessimism she didn't often express. He wasn't getting through to her.

"I'm not perfect and never pretended to be, Tessa, but we're not your parents. I'll say it again—or do you see us suddenly turning into them?"

She didn't answer, but he could see he'd nailed the deep issue that had her seeing only the worst of relationships.

"I think the conversation we should be having," he continued, "is about your parents and the fact that you've never come to terms with this and who they are. They're flawed deeply, and they have no desire to change. They broke every promise to you, disappointed you, and you figured it was easier to do everything yourself. But you haven't now, not for a while. It's been you and me. I'm pretty sure I'm not your father. I don't understand why you're instantly going there, thinking that could be us. Me putting a ring on your finger, us signing a paper and being mister and missus, that doesn't change who we are. Do you not love me?" He tried to smile, but he could see she wasn't impressed.

"I know we're not my parents, and this isn't about them. Now you're being ridiculous. Of course I love you, or we wouldn't be doing this thing, playing house. But what's the rush?" She shrugged, and he could see she wasn't about to shake this twisted view.

"The rush! You're kidding, right? Tessa, we've been living together for over a year—eighteen months, to be exact. The fact is that I wasn't in a hurry either, but you seem to have your standards set so high that no one can meet them. What exactly is it that you expect is going to happen? Am I suddenly going to turn into someone different, like your dad?"

He leaned in, and by the way she flinched, he knew he'd nailed it, that sore spot of hers. For a moment, he wondered if she'd snarl, and he stepped back, lifting his hands in the air, as she pulled her arms around her chest.

"You know who I am, Tessa. I'm not perfect, not by a longshot, but you know things about me I'd never share with anyone. Or is that the problem?"

She looked over to him so sharply, so fast, her blue eyes flashing. "No, Owen, it's not, and you know that.

You know I won't do secrets. I get what happened to you and your family, and I'm just as much a part of it as you are now."

He only nodded as he stepped back, his hands fisted at his sides. He ran one over his hair, letting out a sigh.

She didn't pull her gaze. "You know marriage isn't the answer to everything," she said, and she sounded so reasonable. "What's your hurry, Owen? Why now?"

Again, her voice was so soft, and for a moment, he had to wonder if she wasn't right.

"Because, Tessa, I love you, and I want to have kids, our kids. To me, marriage doesn't seem like the worst thing ever. Maybe I want to tell everyone you're my wife, to just take that next step with you. But I can see from all this that you're not where I am. I have to ask, will you ever be ready, or is it just me you won't marry? I want you to think about it, really, objectively, without your parents' baggage coming into play. Just leave them out of this thing between you and me. Can you do that?"

She jutted her chin and pulled her gaze, and he could see how tense she was. Wow! Just talking about marriage had sent her into a tailspin. Then she shrugged and uncrossed her arms, dragging her gaze back over to him.

Instead of answering, all she did was nod. "I need to get dressed. Can you pack up the vegetables I cut? I promised your mom and Charlotte we'd also bring dessert, which is in the fridge—some pudding for the kids."

As he watched this woman he loved pull on a pair of jeans and run a brush through her hair, he realized she had already shifted her focus to any conversation that didn't include marriage or a future with him.

CHAPTER

Two

"You've been rather distracted of late," Suzanne said. "When you're distracted, you don't talk much, and considering my entire life and our relationship revolves solely around you and what you do…"

"So get a job," Harold cut in rather sharply as he sat on the bed, which now had a gold flowered duvet set and pillows that matched the curtains. Suzanne's current pastime was decorating.

She pushed herself up from where she was lying on her stomach on the bed, her legs kicked up behind her. She didn't know what to make of the way he was watching her. His brown eyes flickered with mischief at times, though the man could be far too serious.

"Or not," he added before she could respond.

"I had a job, a great one," she said, "doing something I really loved—until politics came into play and I was forced out."

Harold unbuttoned his deputy shirt and tossed it into the dirty clothes hamper in the corner, then stepped out of his dark trousers. She knew he'd climb in the shower next, and then they'd head over to Marcus's for family night, tree decorating, and beer, which she hadn't bothered to pick up. Maybe she'd share that fact on the way.

"Suzanne, that was over a year ago, almost two. You can't keep holding on to it. There's a point where you have to let it go and move on. You won't get another job with the department in this county because of Toby and his family, who still decide who works and who doesn't. I'm pretty sure that applies to the surrounding counties, too, because the old boys' blue network has a wide reach. Yes, you were great as a fire-fighter, but you need to look at something else. Or not."

There he went again, offering her nothing. She wondered whether he deliberately avoided telling her what to do, letting her flounder.

"Why do you have to do that?" she said.

He was naked now after tossing his socks and under-wear in the hamper, and she wasn't sure what to make of his face as he shook his head and walked into the ensuite of the very comfortable two-bedroom condo, which was all his, not hers.

She heard the shower and listened to him step in. He hadn't answered her, so she strode into the spacious bathroom, seeing him through the glass shower door. She scanned the freestanding tub they had shared many times and the dual sink. The bathroom was clean, but then, what else did she have to do?

She realized he was looking at her, his head turned even though he'd pressed his hands flat to the tiled wall, the water running down his back, over his head. He swept his hair back, then reached for a bar of soap and ran it over himself.

"Suzanne, are you looking for me to tell you what to do? Is that what this is?"

It would be so easy to say yes, but he had to know how much she didn't like anyone telling her what to do.

He said nothing else, and she heard him sigh. Yeah, he could wait her out, but she really felt as if she were on a tightrope. He'd just gone along and made things easy for her for so long, too long.

"Look, I have no idea what I want to do," she said. "I have a lot of time on my hands, and I can do only so much: clean your place, go shopping, visit my family, wait for you to come home… And when you do, I can always tell when you don't want to talk or share, because you say nothing, and I mean nothing, like now." She gestured toward him, watching as he squeezed shampoo into his hand and washed his short cop cut. He gave the appearance that he wasn't really one hundred percent in this conversation.

"I don't want to talk about work," he said, "and there're some things I can't share. Cases are confidential. You know that."

He rinsed his hair and then turned off the shower, and she reached for the light blue towel and handed it to him as he stepped out. He wasn't as tall as her brothers, but, man, was he hot, sexy, with a body she knew she'd never tire of looking at.

"Honestly, Suzanne, this is starting to sound as if you want me to tell you what to do, to get a job, to do something. So I'm going to just say it, because, frankly, to me, you just being here and happy is all I care about. I just want to see you smile. Really, I don't want you working back in some male-dominated area where you're not appreciated, where you're taken advantage of and not defended, because a bunch of guys would rather look away than step up and deal with the fact that you were disrespected."

He ran the towel over his head and looped it around his waist as he walked over to the sink, then reached for his toothbrush and squeezed toothpaste on it, looking in the mirror at his reflection and then over to her. There was forceful passion in his words when he spoke, and he didn't have to raise his voice.

"I'm happy when you're happy," he said. "I haven't said anything because of what happened to you in the department. It broke every traditional labor law out there, but you'll never get anyone to admit it or do anything about it. You can't fix something that's part of society, a system that has been run the same way since the beginning of time. No one wants it to change. Maybe one day, but we're not there yet. I'd rather you not be the trailblazer, in the line of fire. I just want to see you smile, hear you laugh—and you're right that I'm fine with this, because then I don't have to worry about you. But listening to you now, it's sounding like you're not happy, so do something that will make you happy. That's all I want. Figure out a new occupation you could do that would be safer."

There it was, the one thing she didn't think he'd ever say.

"Safer! Are you saying you have a problem with me being a firefighter?"

"You *were* a firefighter," he said, pulling the toothbrush from his mouth and spitting in the sink. He ran the water and rinsed his toothbrush. "You're no longer one. And if you want me to be honest, yeah, maybe I am happy, because this way I don't have to worry about you getting trapped in some burning building because the men you worked with didn't have your back. If you need a refresher on what happened…"

She made a rude noise and stepped out of the bathroom in her sweats and bare feet, hearing him swear under his breath. His toothbrush clanged as he put it back into the holder.

She took in his spacious master bedroom, feeling the soft light carpeting under her feet. She spent way too much time in this condo. She glanced over her shoulder to see him standing in the doorway now, leaning, his arms crossed over that damn impressive chest.

"You know, Suzanne, the moment I tell you what to do, you'll tell me where to go—and likely give me directions. You're lost, floundering. You think I don't know? I do, but you have to let the fire department go and figure out something else. I mean, look at this place, all this decorating you've done…" He gestured.

She thought he hadn't noticed. Matching and color coordination weren't really on his radar. "Seriously? I just made your place look nice—got matching towels, moved furniture, added features to the living room so it wasn't such a mancave. I was bored, but I'm not a designer, and I don't want to be one. Is that the kind of job that falls into your 'safe' category?"

He lifted his hands as he strode into the bedroom, then pulled open the drawer where his clothes were, also neatly folded because of all the time she had on her hands. He tossed the towel on the bed and stepped into clean underwear, then pulled out black socks and sat on the bed to pull them on.

"Exactly my point," he said. "You really don't want me telling you what to do, Suzanne, so help me out here. Are you just looking to vent and for me to say nothing, or are you wanting me to fix something?"

He looked over to her, his expression serious, as he stood up and said nothing else. He strode back over to the chest of drawers and opened the bottom one to pull out his blue jeans. As he stepped into them, she stared at his back, which was just as impressive as his chest, then took in her own image in the dresser mirror.

Harold pulled on a blue and green T-shirt before closing the drawers and looking over to her. "Suzanne, I can't help if I don't know where your head is."

"Fine. You want to know? Here it is. This condo is yours. Everything in here is yours. I sold my house and paid off the mortgage, so that left me with not much of anything. What I didn't sell of my old furniture I gave to Alison and Brady. I've got nothing that feels like mine, and yeah, I've tried to figure out something else to do, but I honestly feel like a kept woman, and there are times I don't know where we stand."

When she turned around, she didn't think she'd ever seen him so shocked.

"You don't know where we stand?" he said.

Okay, maybe she'd been a little too forthcoming. She leaned back against the dresser and pulled her arms over her chest, knowing Harold wasn't the kind of guy who said the touchy-feely things she wasn't sure she even wanted.

He made a rude noise and started out of the bedroom before turning back in the doorway and gesturing quite forcefully toward her. "I love you, and we're together. Stop picking things apart and creating a problem where there isn't one. Let's go, or would you rather call your brothers and tell them we're not coming? This is for you, Suzanne. Everything I do, I do it for you. Do I have to say it?" He stepped back into the room and gestured widely with his hands. Oh, there it was, the passion, the anger that he never showed. "I hear silence when a few minutes ago, you had tons to say. So which is it, Suzanne, do we go or stay? Or is there something else?" he snapped, his fire now at a slow simmer.

"No, I'm good," she said, then gave him her back, pulled open the drawer, and reached for her jeans. As she pulled them out, she knew he was still standing there, but she didn't look up.

She heard him step out of the bedroom, feeling the edge and the unsettled rift that was beginning to build, all because she, somehow, somewhere along the way, had lost her footing.

CHAPTER

Three

Suzanne took in her work-in-progress MGB under a black tarp in the back parking lot of Harold's condo. Living with Harold and selling her place had meant losing her garage, the only thing about her small old house that she'd liked. What she wouldn't have given to be able to have a garage, to lift the hood and tinker, to check the fluid levels, to play around and get her hands dirty…

"Ah, yeah, that happy place," Suzanne said under her breath with wistful longing, remembering a feeling she hadn't felt in a long time. She wondered whether Harold even understood the part of her that was now missing.

She felt the bite of the cold as her breath fogged the air, and she slid her bare hands into her red down coat pockets as she stood next to Harold's new Kia, fingering the keys. She had driven him to the station so she could drive around his new car today, but they'd ridden in silence.

"Hey, what are you doing back here?" Tessa said, trudging through the snowy parking lot, which still needed to be cleared. She wore a fuzzy white hat with a purple down jacket that stopped just above her knees, with practical heavy black winter boots. "Thought you were going to meet me out front."

"Sorry, had to drive Harold to work, and I was just..." She gestured to her car, her baby, then started walking over to Tessa, who had suggested Christmas shopping today, as she was now on her Christmas break.

Tessa took in the back lot, the tarp over her classic car. "You haven't driven your car in a while. It looks pretty lonely over there."

"Yeah, unfortunately, Montana winters aren't ideal for a classic sporty convertible. Owen at home?" She fell in beside Tessa as they walked back around the front of the building.

"No, he had an emergency call. Seems winter is his busiest time for plumbing emergencies, with frozen pipes. He'll likely be busy all day."

From the way she said it, Suzanne was starting to pick up on something else. "I noticed you and my brother seemed distant last night," she said. "Trouble in paradise?"

Tessa didn't smile, instead lingering with that same off aura she had noticed the night before.

"Did my brother do something?" Suzanne said. "Because, hey, I love him, but Owen is about as pigheaded as they come. Growing up with him as a big brother, I know he's not the easiest..."

"He asked me to marry him," Tessa cut in, unsmiling.

"And you're not jumping up and down? You said no." Suzanne's immediate feeling of joy turned to sorrow.

Tessa shook her head. "I didn't say anything. I'm just not sure I want to get married. I mean, everything is perfect now the way it is, and he wants to go and throw marriage into the mix, to ruin a good thing."

Suzanne just stared at this woman, her family. As she looked at Tessa, she wondered what was going on in her head. At least now she could see why Owen and Tessa had seemed off the night before. She'd thought she was imagining it, with the tension that lingered with her and Harold.

"Why is that? I thought you and Owen were headed that way. You're almost married now. It seems the next logical step." She hoped it wasn't because Tessa wasn't as committed as Owen was. She knew he'd never felt about a woman the way he felt about Tessa.

Tessa let out a heavy sigh that only added to the heaviness that had lingered in Suzanne as of late. "Don't get me wrong: I love Owen, but marriage isn't in my plan, ever. If I were to get married, it would be to Owen, just to be clear, but why marriage? Why now? Everything is perfect. I just don't see the need for it. As you said, we seem almost married. Why isn't that good enough?"

Something about the way she was talking gave Suzanne the sense that Tessa wasn't comfortable with the entire subject. She didn't miss the edge to her voice, and she found herself really looking at Tessa, wondering how she hadn't known this about her. For whatever reason, she'd always just assumed that Tessa and Owen were absolutely perfect. Apparently, she didn't have any idea. But then, the same could've been said of her and Harold.

"Because he wants more," Suzanne said. "He wants it with you, Tessa. I can see that much. Owen is steady…"

"You think I don't know that? It's not about that. It's just that I don't understand why marriage seems to be the next step in the natural evolution of a relationship. I don't need a piece of paper to say, okay, I've made the ultimate sacrifice to show that I love him. I already do—and if you really want to get into the nitty gritty, getting married actually costs you money. Being married puts you in a different tax bracket, and when the tax man comes calling, you have to pay more in taxes, a lot more. It's no wonder so many stay single, live together, and be roommates. Legally, that piece of paper costs money. Married people find themselves broke, struggling, arguing, fighting…"

Tessa had stopped walking. The way her face lit up as she spoke, it was as if she'd just figured out the problem with the world.

"So this is about money, then?" Suzanne said. She had never figured Tessa to be so focused on the negative, pinching pennies.

Tessa made a face and shrugged. "I guess that sounded a little ridiculous."

All Suzanne could do was wonder where Tessa really stood. "Just a little crazy. If you're having cold feet and freaking out because of marriage, just say so," she said, and for a moment, it seemed as if she'd finally found Tessa's sore spot.

"Fine. I have issues with marriage. Are you happy?"

The way Tessa looked at her, she could see fear and something else. Her brother had his work cut out for him.

She shrugged where they stopped by the car, taking in a poster attached to the utility pole. It was a photo of a black man, and above it was the word *pedophile* in red. A sudden heaviness had her reading the flyer, taking in every detail, feeling the shock.

"Did you see this?" she said, stepping closer, taking in the image of a young man she thought she'd never seen before. His address was just up the street, and all she could think of was Eva and Cameron. Again, that sick heavy feeling seemed to really weigh on her. "Great, so we have a pedophile living in the area."

Tessa was reading the poster and the personal details about the man. "It looks like someone is looking after the neighborhood and has taped posters all up the street. Remind me to thank whoever it was."

All Suzanne could think of was calling Harold to tell him and ask for details: who, what, where, and how. Better yet, she wanted to find a way to get him out of town.

Just up the street, someone else seemed to be ripping the posters down.

"Tessa, look…" She tapped her arm, gesturing toward him. "Do you think that's him, this Nathan Rand?"

She took in the name and then the man. He looked about her height, in baggy clothes and a hoodie pulled up with a down vest over it. She couldn't see his face, just his back. She took a step toward him, but Tessa slapped her arm, pulling her back.

"What are you doing?" she snapped.

Suzanne looked back to see the panic that was suddenly there. "Going to have a word with him." She gestured as she went to take another step, but Tessa was holding on to her and pulling her back.

"Are you crazy! No, you're not going to talk to him. If that's him, a pedophile, then you'd do right to stay away from him, far away!"

"Nonsense. I'm just having a word. I used to do this kind of thing. It's fine. If it's him, I'm just going to set him straight on a few things." She took another step, feeling Tessa still pulling on her arm. Damn, she was strong.

"No, no, no! This is crazy, Suzanne. Let's go. Come on, just get in the car—or, better yet, call that man of yours, you know, the deputy who does this for a living. Let him handle this."

She just shook her head, letting out a rude noise under her breath, and kept moving, pulling on Tessa. "Seriously, Tessa? As someone who's against marriage, you want me to call Harold to come and rescue us? I think not." She really dug into each step.

Tessa was still holding her arm. Suzanne felt for the first time in a long time that she was doing something, in control of something, taking charge of a situation. She hadn't had the opportunity since being bounced from the fire department.

"Excuse me," she called out.

It was clear the posters had been tacked and taped to every post and pole on the street. Someone had really taken it upon him- or herself to expose this man, but the closer she got, she realized it wasn't a man but a woman. She had a scar on her chin, and her dark eyes seemed to blend in with her skin. She was holding the flyers, and her face told a tale of outrage and emotion.

Suzanne still felt the weight of Tessa on her arm. At the same time, she couldn't remember the last time she'd felt so in control. She really missed handling situations the average person couldn't.

"Why are you taking down these flyers?" she said, stopping right in front of the woman, who she thought had to be her age.

"This smear campaign, is this your doing?" the woman snarled, fisting the flyer with the photo of a young man on it.

Suzanne felt the punch. "No, I have no idea who put it up, but if there is a pedophile in the area, the community needs to know. There are kids here. Seriously, stop. Why are you ripping them down?"

"Pedophile! It's amazing, the stories people can spin. You put that label on someone, and people immediately jump to the worst. This is my brother, and he doesn't deserve this, bitch, so get the hell away from me."

Suzanne had to fight the urge to step back from the force of the woman, her words. Anger was rolling off her in waves.

"Suzanne, call Harold," Tessa whispered loudly, squeezing her arm.

She just stared at the woman, who'd said she was the sister of this Rand character. The woman walked around Suzanne and over to another pole, then ripped the flyer off. Suzanne tried to shake off Tessa's hold on her arm, because she was really digging in, panicked.

"No, I'm not calling Harold," she said. "I've got this. Trust me. We don't need a man to come in and handle this."

She'd always been good with talking to people, victims at fire scenes, handling unruly people in crowd control. This was just one woman.

"Look, I'm not your enemy, here, but at the same time, I'm not comfortable having a convicted pedophile around. We have every right to know who it is so we can protect our kids."

The woman was still walking, ripping flyers down. "He didn't molest anyone!" she snapped over her shoulder, tearing up the papers.

"Suzanne, seriously, call Harold or I will," Tessa said, leaning in again, urgency in her voice.

Suzanne just shook her head, and she felt Tessa pull her hand off and step away, her phone out. Evidently, she was calling him herself.

The woman kept walking. She was a little on the overweight side, her blue jeans were worn and faded, and she was wearing sneakers.

"What do you mean, he didn't molest anyone? The flyer says he's a pedophile. Is someone messing with him?"

"Just because someone says something, that doesn't mean it's true," the woman said, ripping off another flyer and walking away again.

Suzanne glanced back to see Tessa on her cell phone. She could hear her tone but not what she was saying. She was upset and agitated, apparently. Someone would be on the way. Great! She had to jog to catch up to the woman.

"Are you saying someone took a picture of your brother and wrote that he's a pedophile, and it's not true? That's horrible."

The woman made a face, and she thought she was

going to push her aside as Suzanne went to help her, her hand touching the flyer, but the woman ripped it from her.

"Why would someone do that to him?"

The woman was walking again at a fast pace. Suzanne didn't have a clue what her name was, but she didn't think she'd forget the image of her brother or his name.

"Look, it's not what you think," she said. "He did his time."

Suzanne stilled, hearing the siren and spotting the flashing lights. She stared at the woman, who pulled another flyer from a tree. "He did his time…like, jail? So he is a convicted pedophile."

The woman stopped, her expression filled with the kind of anger that told Suzanne to take a step back. The warning was there, and she knew it well.

She heard the door and spotted another flash of lights, another cop car coming, and there was Harold walking her way.

"You know, I don't know why I'm trying to explain this to you," the woman said. "My brother did his time, but he's not a pedophile. His only crime was falling for a piece of trash, a high school crush. She was his girl-friend, but that didn't stop him from getting put on a list and being hunted forever like a monster."

"What's going on here?" Harold called out, striding toward her and Rand's sister, who was staring at him with the same kind of hate. A second cop car had arrived, her brother Marcus, and the entire scene was turning into a gong show. The woman gripped the flyers, and Suzanne knew her mouth was gaping.

"Just taking these down," the woman said. "Is there a crime in that? Like, what the hell is this?"

Harold gestured toward the flyers. For a moment, Suzanne didn't think the woman would hand them over. She didn't miss Tessa running over to Marcus, who was now getting out of his sheriff's cruiser, both lights still flashing. Doors across the street opened, and she was pretty sure people were now looking out their windows.

Suzanne took in Harold staring at the flyer. "She said that's her brother, and someone put these flyers up everywhere."

He just shook his head. "Your brother is Nathan Rand?"

From the way he asked, Suzanne wanted to step in.

The woman crossed her arms. "He is, and he didn't ask to be harassed like this. You think this is fair, someone tacking up flyers all up and down the neighborhood with his photo on there, my address, his personal details? He just moved here for a clean start. He doesn't deserve this." She gave her full hundred-watt attitude to him.

"If your brother is on the sex offender registry," Harold said, "he needs to register with us when he moves to town. Don't remember him showing up to do that."

She wanted to pull Harold aside, knowing that Tessa was now standing with Marcus. She could hear her talking but not what she was saying, and she didn't know why she suddenly felt dizzy, hearing the woman arguing with Harold over her brother.

"Suzanne, you okay?" Tessa was right there now as Suzanne stumbled a bit, feeling Harold grip her arm, his strength.

She pulled in a breath as the wave of dizziness passed, and she gave her head a shake. She couldn't remember feeling that lightheaded before.

"Whoa, whoa, Suzanne, what the hell?" Harold had his arm around her. "What's going on here? You almost fell over."

She just shook her head, seeing the woman, whose name she still didn't know, staring at her, and Tessa too. Marcus was also there, and he now held the flyers.

"I'm fine," she said. "I just didn't eat breakfast, is all. My blood sugar must be low."

Harold was still holding her arm, looking at her intently, before he dragged his gaze back to the woman. "Tell your brother to show up at the station by day's end and register, or I'll come looking for him, and he'll find himself back behind bars," he said.

"So you aren't going to do anything about whoever is putting up the flyers? I don't want some angry mob showing up on my doorstep."

Marcus was shaking his head. "Nope, we can't. Just make sure your brother shows up."

So that was it.

The woman just stood there, taking in the scene. "Well, screw you cops," she finally said, then snatched the flyers from Marcus and started walking.

Her brother took a step.

"Let her go, seriously," Suzanne snapped. There was something about this entire situation that left her with a sick feeling in her stomach, and lightheaded, which she never was. "I think I need to sit down for a minute, have some juice and something to eat."

As she took in the two cop cars, Harold and her brother, and Tessa looking at her, all Suzanne could think about was the woman walking the other way, pulling down flyers. She couldn't help wondering, what the hell was Nathan's story?

CHAPTER

Four

Pulling up in front of his mom's house, Owen could see who was there based on all the vehicles. It appeared to be everyone, including Tessa.

He took in the familiar house he'd grown up in and knew like the back of his hand, and he took a second while climbing out of his plumbing van, feeling gritty and running his hand over his face, hearing the scrape of his whiskers. He likely should have stopped at home first and showered, but he probably wouldn't have shown up then.

There were days he was tired, but today it was cold that went through him. He was having Brady crawl into holes and under houses now, since he was younger and Owen hated that part of the job. He much preferred standing and telling the kid what to do.

He pulled at the knit cap he still wore and took in his hands, which were covered in grime, then kept walking up the driveway, which was cleared of snow to the front door. He could see the decorated Christmas tree through the front window and hear everyone's voices inside before he opened the door and stomped the snow off his boots.

He spotted the playpen set up in the living room and Cameron in there with a pile of toys. Luke was on the sofa with a beer, and Marcus too, whereas Harold, Suzanne, and Raymond, a.k.a. Jake, were in the living room, conversing. He wondered whether he'd ever feel something other than disillusionment when facing the man who was his father.

Of course, he nodded to him. He wasn't sure what was up as he kicked off his boots, hearing voices from the kitchen, as well.

"Well, you look like you stepped into it," Luke called out. "Brady said you had a hell of a job today."

Owen took a second to stare at Luke, who was sporting a short, really neat haircut. He couldn't remember the last time he'd seen his brother so polished.

Tessa walked in, holding two beers. Her blue eyes were hesitant, distant, and her long blond hair was in a loose single braid. He didn't have a clue where he stood with her, exactly, or how to address this thing she didn't want to talk about.

"This time of year is always when I need the extra help, because this is when problems people have ignored present themselves. Frozen pipes are the worst."

Tessa was holding a beer out to him. He glanced in the mirror on the closet door. Maybe he really should have gone home first and changed. He shrugged off his heavy coat, and Tessa reached for it, took it from him, and stepped closer.

"Here, take this. I'll hang it up," she said.

He took the beer and hesitated a second, seeing something in her expression, something that softened for him. He leaned in and kissed her. Her hand was on his face, her thumb running over his day-old beard.

"Hmm," was all she said. Then she stepped away and hung up his coat, and he stepped down into the living room.

He took in Suzanne, who was lounging in the chair in the living room, wearing sweatpants and a white and blue sweatshirt. It seemed he'd walked in on something. No one said anything, everyone looking at him as he pulled off his knitted hat and tossed it on a chair, then ran his fingers through hair he knew was likely sticking up.

"So…" he said, gesturing with his beer, waiting for someone to say something.

Harold was standing, and he jutted his chin to Owen, whereas Raymond sat on the ottoman, his forearms on his knees. Marcus sat at the other end of the sofa with a groan. The Christmas tree was lit up, with more gifts wrapped underneath.

"What's going on?" Owen said, again gesturing with his beer. "Did I miss something?"

Tessa appeared beside him. "Something happened today when I went to pick up Suzanne."

"I guess I just don't understand why you're both being so hard-headed about this," Suzanne cut in, looking at Harold and Marcus.

He wasn't sure what to make of Luke's expression, the way he just shook his head. Harold was looking down on Suzanne, and Owen would've been blind to miss the tension that lingered.

"It's not about me being hard-headed, Suzanne,"

Harold snapped. "The law's the law. I don't make the laws or write them, but I do have to enforce them. If you don't like it, then write the congressman and get him to change it."

Owen realized he really had walked into the middle of something, a problem between Harold and Suzanne. He dragged his gaze over and down to Tessa. "So what gives? What happened?" he asked.

"There were flyers on posts and trees all up and down my street," Suzanne said just as Tessa opened her mouth to speak. "It was a photo of a young black man, with *pedophile* written in red. It had all his personal details, the address where he's living on our street. Apparently, he's living with his sister, who was out there ripping them all down. She was pissed."

"You have a pedophile on your street? What the hell are you doing about it?" Owen said. He knew he sounded accusing. He gave everything to Harold and then Marcus, but, from the way his brother inclined his head, he suspected there was more. Way more.

"Not according to the sister," Suzanne said. "I asked her. Was talking to her, just getting to the bottom of it, when Tessa had to call Harold, and then both Harold and Marcus showed up, sirens blasting as if there was a crisis, creating quite a scene—as if someone had been killed or something. I still can't believe you called Harold." Suzanne glared at Tessa, accusing.

He'd seen this look before from Suzanne, though this was a side of her he hadn't seen in a long time. She was looking for a fight.

"What? Wait a second," Owen said. "Hang on. Are you telling me you walked into the middle of trouble?"

"Oh my God, Owen, are you serious? I'm not some

helpless damsel who needs a man to rescue me." Suzanne was really on a roll. She leaned forward, ready to do battle, and Harold lifted his gaze to the ceiling as if he'd already been down this road with her. "I was just getting to the bottom of it. She was furious. She said her brother didn't do it."

"He was charged and convicted, Suzanne," Marcus finally said quite sharply, a loud and bossy edge to his voice. "He did his time. He's on the sex offender registry, and he's required to show up and register here, which he didn't do."

Owen spotted Charlotte lifting Cameron out of the playpen and taking him into the kitchen, where everyone else was congregating. The mama bear didn't want Cameron hearing this debacle.

" I get what you're saying," Marcus continued, "but you don't get to choose how this plays out. The courts already did. You heard Harold. If you don't like the way the law works, write our congressman, because I'm not going back and forth on this with you. You think the law is fair? It sucks, and there are parts of it I really hate. Maybe he got screwed. I don't know. I'm not looking into something that happened in another state."

"Are we getting to the point yet?" Owen said.

Marcus dragged in a breath. Owen looked down at Tessa, who seemed on edge, as if there were more. Maybe she'd already received a tongue-lashing from Suzanne, who seemed the easygoing one until she wasn't.

"Sure," Suzanne said. "Why don't you both explain to Owen why a black kid from Indiana dating a white girl a year younger than him in high school now carries the title of pedophile forever? He turned eighteen while she was still seventeen, and he was charged with statutory rape and went to jail for it. I think everyone here should be horrified and outraged. She was his girlfriend. Isn't that what you said, Harold? Come on—and the way you two talked to his sister as if she were a common criminal when she's just looking for some peace for her brother. Now some asshole in the neighborhood is making sure they don't get a break."

Owen wasn't sure where to look.

Harold leveled a pretty hard gaze at Suzanne. "You're not a cop, Suzanne, so Tessa was completely right in calling us. You overstepped. Yeah, you're right, he was screwed, but it was Indiana. He wasn't about to get a fair shake there. It shouldn't have happened, but it did, probably because of who the girl's father was. I can almost guess how it played out. He knew the law and made enough noise, and the kid was charged and labeled a sex offender because he fell for the wrong girl. Again, I don't make the law, but the way it's written, she was a minor, so he's forever categorized with all those kiddie-porn pedophiles. Nathan Rand has to register here. I didn't say it was fair, so let it go."

"You looked into his case?" Marcus said, sounded so accusing as he dragged his gaze to Harold. It seemed there could be a lot more friction in this house before the end of the night.

"She hounded me," Harold said, sounding as if he'd been cornered. "What was I supposed to do?"

Owen stared down at his little sister, who he knew could stir things up and wouldn't let things go. He knew Harold likely hadn't had a choice.

"Tell her no," Marcus said, so matter of fact.

Suzanne lifted her hands in the air and stood up.

Owen thought she'd say something to Marcus, but all she did was level him with the kind of look he wouldn't have wanted directed his way. Then she turned to Owen and wrinkled her nose. "Man, you stink, Owen," she said before striding out of the room and into the kitchen.

For a minute, he sympathized with Harold. He didn't think he smelled that bad.

Tessa just shook her head and tapped his arm. "She's been off all day, kind of moody, ever since this run-in."

"Is that true about the young man?" Owen said. He took in Luke and Raymond, who had been relatively quiet.

"Unfortunately," Raymond said. "I heard it happens. In fact, when I met Iris, she was only seventeen, and I was a few years older. Today, it's a problem. If anyone had any idea that half the men in America could've ended up on a list… The law was never meant for something like this."

Owen didn't know what to say. "So it was a simple one-year age difference, two kids having sex, or was it something more?"

"I pulled the case file in the database," Harold said, then pulled in a breath. "I know, Marcus, but your sister wasn't going to drop it. From what I read, the girl's father pushed for the charges. She never made a statement or came forward. This was a small Indiana county where Rand didn't stand a chance. It read like 1950s-style justice. There was a brief note from Rand that she was his girlfriend, but then, the sheriff told a different story. If you read between the lines, it looks like the girl's father didn't like the color of Rand's skin and didn't take kindly to his hands on his daughter. A judge signed off on it, and the kid did four years. He's been out for two and has had to move seven times. You know, when communities find out, a witch hunt forms. He'll have that label forever. He's screwed."

"And now someone's putting up flyers," Owen said, trying to understand what was going on, very aware this was the first time he'd ever seen Marcus so quiet. "So let me guess: The harassment will start, the threats, never giving that family a peaceful moment, until someone takes matters into his own hands or he moves on."

"If a problem happens and they call, we'll show up just like we would for anyone else," was all Marcus said.

Owen found himself taking in his sister's back. She was now sitting on a stool at the island in the kitchen with Charlotte, Jenny, Ryan, his mom, and Cassie. Something about his sister seemed more off than usual tonight.

Owen followed Tessa home to a house that was hers and had always been hers. He'd never understood until now, but her need to be in control was an invisible roadblock between them.

He pulled into the driveway beside her light blue compact and parked, then took his time getting out, well aware that she was now standing beside the car, waiting for him. He wasn't sure what to make of her unease. Was it that they wanted opposite things in their relationship, or was it that family night had been filled with rifts and tension?

It seemed as if everyone and everything was off tonight. He hadn't noticed such tension before between Suzanne and Harold, especially. Maybe he needed to pay closer attention, or maybe he needed to have a one on one with his sister and find out what was up with her.

"I can see you're still pretty angry with me," Tessa said, her hands in her coat pockets. He didn't have to touch her to feel how tense and on edge she was.

"I'm not angry, Tessa. I'm just tired. Let's go in. It's cold," he said, knowing he sounded short.

He followed Tessa into the house, looking out at the darkened street, which was quiet. The streetlamps offered little light. It was cold, and he wanted a hot shower.

He closed the door and waited for Tessa to hang up her coat and pull off her boots, then toss her hat and gloves into a drawer of the bench by the front door. Owen kicked off his boots, slipped off his coat, and reached for a hanger.

"I'm going to make some tea," she said. "Do you want some?"

He just shook his head as he pulled the closet door closed, taking in the darkened living room, where he still needed to finish the brickwork around the fireplace hearth.

"Could you actually talk to me, or is this all I'm going to get?" Tessa said. "The silent treatment, a nod, maybe a grunt. You say you're not angry with me, but I can see you are. You have this way about you, Owen, when someone does something you don't like, and I've very well aware—"

"Stop it, would you?" He cut her off, hearing how sharply it came out.

She pulled back, standing there in the open kitchen as if he'd slapped her.

"Sorry," he said. "You're misreading me. I'm tired right now, and having an entire debate or talking about my feelings is not something I want to do. I want to shower and go to bed, because I have to be back at the job site in the morning to deal with a plumbing nightmare all because the owner decided to cut corners and didn't properly insulate the lines coming into the house. Now the family he rents to are stuck without water.

"I had to listen to a day of excuses from the land-lord, nickel and diming me to death because he wanted a cost breakdown before letting me fix one thing. I had to threaten the guy and say I was leaving and not coming back if he didn't cut the bullshit, yet he argued with me every step of the way, suggesting I could just patch it instead of doing what was necessary. You can't patch plumbing!

"So it's not you, Tessa. It's me having to deal with an idiot all day today and tomorrow, as well, and the fact that I'll likely have to chase the asshole around to get paid. Don't automatically assume I'm angry with you. I'm disappointed you don't want to get married. What I want is marriage, but you don't. Then there's my sister and this incident you were involved in. It sounds like it could have the potential to escalate and turn ugly.

"Suzanne has always been pigheaded, walking into things as if she's invincible. She's the one in the family where something could be going on and you won't have a clue until it's about to blow up. She's always been good at hiding things, keeping everyone in the dark…"

As he stepped into the hallway, Tessa firmed her lips and pulled her arms over her chest, the cream-colored sweater he hadn't really noticed. Her hair was hanging long and loose. He pulled off his hat and gave it a toss onto the bench by the door, then made himself walk until he stood right in front of her. He let out a sigh, and she flicked those blue eyes up to him, those eyes that had a way of reaching inside him, touching him like no one ever could.

"I'm scared," she said. She glanced away, her arms still crossed.

He touched the side of her head, her hair, and she leaned into his palm. "I see that, but I don't know of what. I'm not suddenly going to change, Tessa. But only you can figure out this baggage you're carrying about what you think marriage means. If you think getting married to me is somehow going to change who we are, then I don't think you're giving me enough credit. Getting married isn't a death sentence. I want you, but not like this…"

He could see her thinking. Then she reached out and pressed her hand over his chest, touching his black long-sleeved knit. He knew she could feel the thump of his heart.

"So you're okay about not getting married," she said.

He didn't know what to say as he rested his hands over hers. "No, I want to get married. I haven't changed my mind. I want to have kids. I already told you how I feel, but I'm not sure how to convince you of something I want. Right here, with this, I can see you're not ready. Maybe you never will be, Tessa."

She pulled her hands from under his grip, and he could see this was fast turning into the same argument, or maybe she'd just walk away. "You know, your sister is pretty angry with me," she said.

There she went, changing the subject. Apparently, that was all she was prepared to say to him on the subject of their future. Right, he could push her only so far, and he could see the minute the subject was closed. He couldn't help the sigh that passed his lips.

"Suzanne is Suzanne," he said. "She was off tonight.

I plan on having a word with her. I wouldn't take it personally, though. I'm pretty sure it was the circumstances, is all. At the same time, I'm not too happy to hear that you two almost got tangled up in something. I'm going to take a shower."

He didn't wait for Tessa to respond as he started down the hallway to their bedroom.

"Look, Suzanne wouldn't let it go," Tessa said. "I'm actually horrified to hear the situation with this young man, but I'm not sure how I feel, Owen. I've never seen her just go head to head with someone like that, right in her face. I would never want to be on that side of her. It could have turned into something really bad. Maybe I overreacted, but I didn't know the story. Now, hearing it, I'm still not sure what to feel. Maybe there's more that we don't know. I mean, seriously, he was charged, after all."

Owen pulled off his shirt and tossed it on top of the pile of dirty clothes in the already full hamper. He figured he should probably throw a load of clothes in before bed. As he sat on the bed and pulled off his heavy socks, even Tessa made a face.

"I've heard about wrongful convictions enough from Marcus, but I've also heard him say sexual assault is a significant problem. Even if the policy is based on a misconception, if I were you, I'd stay out of it. You don't know the man's story."

Tessa seemed to consider what he was saying, then shook her head. "Suzanne was right. You probably should've showered before you came over. You know, that's another thing. She wasn't feeling well today, which has me wondering if that's why she blew up the way she did. She said she hadn't eaten breakfast. She almost passed out, lost her balance, when shit hit the fan and Harold and Marcus showed up. We never did end up going shopping. Suzanne had a bite to eat, and I left, because she and Harold were getting into it about that Rand character…" She pressed her hand to the bridge of her nose, frustrated.

"Suzanne's pigheaded," he said. "She takes nothing lying down, another of her deceptive traits. She seems to be this happy, easygoing person when she's really complicated and difficult. I almost feel for Harold on this one. Again, I'll check in with her."

Tessa was standing there now, her arms crossed. The way she stared at him, the way her brow furrowed, he could see he was in for something. "You know, Owen, Suzanne isn't your responsibility anymore. She's a grown woman. I can't help thinking of Harold and how he likely wouldn't appreciate you stepping into the middle of this thing between them."

He stood up from the bed so Tessa had to look up at him. "She's my sister, Tessa. If Harold has a problem with me checking in, then he needs to get over it. My family is always my responsibility; that's what being in a family means. You think I'm just going to sit back if Suzanne is in trouble or hasn't got her head screwed on straight?" He shook his head, stepping closer to Tessa, looking down at her. He could feel how unsettled she was, ready to argue, ready to fight.

"And let me guess: Only you can fix it. Is that what you're saying?" she said. There it was, the fire in her.

"This isn't about that—but she's my sister. Just because she and Harold are together, that doesn't mean I'm going to suddenly take a back seat. It goes without saying that if anyone in my family needs me, I'll step in.

I've always done it. You're right that they're not little kids, but she's my sister, and that means we're always in each other's lives, no matter what. If she's in trouble, if she has a problem, yeah, I'm sticking my nose in."

Tessa's eyes widened. "Well, I wonder how Harold would feel if he heard you planning to interfere in his and Suzanne's business. It would be kind of like one of your siblings stepping into this thing between you and me."

He couldn't help the laugh that rumbled low in his chest, but she didn't seem amused. "If they could figure out how to make some sense stick in that stubborn, thick head of yours, I'd tell them to come on in and have at you."

She gasped, outraged, but he only stepped back, unzipped his jeans, and tossed them on the heap of dirty clothes before starting into the bathroom.

Instead of saying anything or telling him where to go, all Tessa did was lift her hands in the air, make a rude noise under her breath, and walk out of the bedroom.

"Well, you handled that well, O'Connell," he said under his breath as he turned on the shower and stepped in, knowing that instead of smoothing anything over with Tessa, he'd managed to ensure a rather quiet and chilly night next to her in bed.

CHAPTER

Six

The sun was bright today. Suzanne vaguely remembered Harold leaning down and kissing her cheek, showered, dressed, and saying he'd call her later, then leaving her housebound, asleep and careless. It was after nine when she finally woke up and climbed out of bed. It had been quite a while since she'd slept in.

She still felt there was a lot Harold hadn't answered, and she just couldn't shake this sense of injustice that she'd never felt before. After she took a long shower and dried her hair, she stared in the mirror at her complexion—her unblemished light skin, her blue eyes, her hair the same old brown.

She realized she didn't have a clue what she wanted, what she needed, but staying here within four walls, day in and day out, was likely why she was feeling so unsettled. All she wanted was to do something important, just like Harold, who seemed to have something she never would.

"Right…" she said to herself as she leaned on the

counter, looking at her image for another second before stepping out of the bathroom, seeing the bed she hadn't bothered to make yet. She pulled open the dresser and reached for her favorite blue jeans, but when she stepped into them and pulled them up, she felt how snug they were, and she couldn't do them up.

"Okay, shit! Seriously, Suzanne, this is ridiculous. Now you're putting on weight?"

She stared in the dresser mirror, seeing how tight her jeans were, and she wondered when the extra pounds had started. Right, that was what happened when she lived in sweats every day and wasn't carrying firehoses up and down a ladder.

She took her jeans off and tossed them on the bed, then pulled on dark navy sweatpants and a white sweatshirt, feeling the comfort but also suspecting that this routine she had somehow slipped into had to go. Today was the day she would figure it out.

She strode into the kitchen, suddenly feeling as if the simple shift in perspective was everything. She flicked on the kettle, taking in the plate and mug Harold had left for her to clean in the sink. That was another thing they'd slipped into, her picking up after him.

She lifted her gaze, looking out the window over the sink, only to see a woman outside, walking down the street, tacking up posters on the trees and posts. She found herself looking harder. The woman wore a red scarf and matching hat and a white coat with a fur collar, walking with purpose. So she was who had put up all the flyers the day before.

She hurried to the front door and shoved her feet in her boots, then pulled on her navy winter coat from the closet and grabbed a wool hat from the bin. She reached for her keys before hurrying out of the second-floor condo and pulling the door closed behind her, locking up quickly.

She spotted the elevator but turned right and took the stairs instead, hurrying down, and she slapped the bar on the exit door to the parking lot. She hurried around the building and had to stop for a second when she couldn't see her.

Damn, she was too slow.

She dragged her gaze first right up the block and then left, seeing cars but not the red coat, which would have stuck out. Then she spotted her across the street at a black Volkswagen, the hatchback open, flyers in her hand.

Suzanne was already crossing the street, looking both ways, seeing the handful of flyers in the woman's hand as she stopped to tack one to a tree.

"Excuse me. What are you doing?" Suzanne called out, seeing the same flyer with Nathan Rand and the word *pedophile* in red, the exact same flyer, just like the day before.

The woman stopped, holding the stapler and flyers, and looked directly at Suzanne. Her hair was shoulder length, thick blond, and styled, from what she could see under her red hat. She wore a huge diamond wedding ring, and her face had a heavy coating of makeup.

"Doing my civic duty as a parent. Did you know a pedophile has moved into the neighborhood? Here. You should take one of these and make sure you tell everyone you know. I mean, this is outrageous, how someone like that can move right in. There are families, kids. How can this be allowed? There should be laws to prevent this." She was holding a paper out to Suzanne, who kept her hands in her pockets.

"Yes, I saw these yesterday before they were taken down."

The woman's face told of her outrage. "By who? I couldn't believe it when my friend texted me to say every one had been taken down. Now I have to waste my time putting them back up. But I will protect the public and get the word out. Here. Can I give you a few to put up in places, let people know?" The woman rifled through the stack of papers and went to hand some to Suzanne, who finally lifted her hand.

"No. Look, I'm not sure you have the right information. When I saw this yesterday, I was outraged, but then I found out the truth. It was the sister of the young man who was taking them down. She was upset and rightfully so. It seems the situation was that a girl's father didn't want Mr. Rand dating his daughter. Both were teenagers. He's not a child molester. He didn't get a fair shake."

The woman stiffened and settled the papers she'd been trying to hand her back into the pile she was holding. "A fair shake? It's a sex crime. He's on the registry for crimes against a child, in case you missed that part. There's no room for any sympathy here. There are lines you don't cross, and he did. He's a sicko, and he's not wanted here. If he knows what's good for him, he'd best move on."

At the way the woman spoke, she could feel her back tense. She had to roll her shoulders. As the woman went to step around her, Suzanne actually took a step to block her way.

"Look, it's not that simple or cut and dried," she

said. "He only wants peace. I think we should give him that. I mean, all you're doing is stirring up a lot of fear and misinformation. If you actually read the charges, what really happened…"

"I don't have to read about what happened. He was charged, and now he's out on the loose, just another predator who shouldn't be allowed on the streets, ever." The woman actually snarled and leaned in.

"So, what, you want to embarrass him and harass his sister, who he lives with? You posted their personal information, their address, everything, so people can show up at their house and start harassing them? Is that your plan, to make it so very uncomfortable for him that he's forced to move? How would you even get a hold of this kind of information, his address, his phone number, where he works…?"

The woman was holding the flyers to her chest. Her face gave Suzanne the impression she wasn't about to hear her out. She knew well when someone had her mind made up.

"Please move out of my way," the woman said. "He's a child molester. He has no rights. So, if he knows what's best for him, he'd better move on out. I mean, the last thing we need here is to worry that someone like him is watching our kids. Why should we have to keep our kids locked up at home when it should be the other way around? With the likes of this monster on the loose, we have to worry that something could happen to one of our kids because of him. Now, I'm not going to ask you again. Please move."

The woman was so direct. She wasn't hearing Suzanne, and she went to step around her.

Suzanne reached for her wrist, grabbing it. "Look,

stop. You're not hearing me. All you're doing is creating a witch hunt. Didn't you hear me when I said he was wrongly and unfairly charged for something that was—"

"Get your hands off me. Now."

Suzanne stepped back, and the woman moved around her and over to the mailbox, where she pulled out tape from her pocket. Her hands had to be cold, but she continued to tape the flyer to the back of the mailbox.

Suzanne couldn't help herself. She walked over, grabbed the flyer, and ripped it off.

The woman gasped. "Stop that right now! Give that back."

Suzanne realized she was talking with someone who had blinders on, who was convinced of something that wasn't true. What was the point in trying to have a conversation with someone who was already convinced? There was nothing she could do to get her to see there was another side.

"You're hurting someone who doesn't deserve this," she said, trying to urge herself to have empathy for someone who was really pissing her off.

"And you're protecting someone who hurts kids. What is your name?" the woman demanded, pulling out a pen from her pocket.

Suzanne realized she was seriously going to write it down. "Why, so you can put my name up too?"

The woman pulled her cell phone from her pocket and held it up, then took a photo of her and pulled it away, a smug expression on her face.

"Hey, I never gave you permission to take my photo," Suzanne said. She went to reach for the phone, but the woman pulled back, smiling at her as if she'd just won the pissing contest. "You delete that photo right now!"

But all the woman did was shake her head, then tuck her phone back into her pocket.

Suzanne tackled her.

Papers flew. She had the woman on the ground, screaming and yelling. Then someone pulled her off, and she heard sirens in the distance.

There was the woman from yesterday, Rand's sister, staring at her.

She heard someone yell that he'd called the cops, and she shook off the hand of a man who pulled her back. The blonde was still yelling her outrage, being helped up by a man and a woman.

Suddenly, she realized what she'd done. People were staring at her as if she'd lost her mind, and in that moment, it hit her that she may have gone a little too far.

"Are you crazy?" Harold snapped, in her face, standing so close.

Suzanne knew Marcus was talking to the other woman, the crazed blonde, whom she still wanted to go another round with. She'd never strayed from a fight or hesitated when she needed to get in someone's face, but she didn't remember ever wanting to fight someone the way she did this woman.

"Look, just ask her," Suzanne said. "She was being an absolute bitch, being unreasonable. I tried to reason with her, but she's the one sticking up all these flyers, trying to stir up things and form a lynch mob who'll show up on his doorstep and chase him out of town. She wouldn't listen when I tried to set her straight on the facts—"

"That's not your place!" he yelled.

Harold had never yelled at her before. He had her arm, steering her away from the crowd that had formed. She noted the phones out, filming the entire thing. Great, she was likely going to be posted online forever for everyone to see, likely with obscured and distorted facts.

"You attacked her," Harold said. "She's demanding you be arrested for assault. This isn't helping, Suzanne. She has the right to notify anyone of a sex offender in the area."

"She's putting up flyers with his personal information, his photo, his address, on every tree, post, and mailbox, and on people's windshields, too. She's littering, creating a frenzy. He's just trying to live in peace. You well know, after checking, that this guy shouldn't be on that list."

"Oh, let me stop you right there. He's on the list because he was convicted of a crime that puts you on the list. The details aren't going to matter, and that's not the point here. I'm not here to retry a case or clear his name. I need to uphold law and order. Right now, this is about you attacking a woman. I have witnesses here, Suzanne, who are all saying you were the aggressor. People are seeing her as the hero, the family watchdog, protecting the interests of the community, and you're the bully on the wrong side. What the hell are you doing, creating a problem, starting a fight with someone? You seriously tackled her? I can't believe this."

He actually put his hands on his face and dragged them down, looking around as if trying to figure out how to talk to her. Then he had his hand back on her arm, moving her further off to the side. He was strong, and she could feel how pissed off he was. Someone she'd never seen before was picking up the flyers scattered everywhere. At least the flashing lights of the cop cars were turned off, but it seemed the spotlight was still on her.

"I just reacted," Suzanne said. "She was being an absolute bitch. She demanded my name, likely to report me, or maybe to create a flyer about me and post it everywhere, with my photo alongside his. By the way, she also took my photo without my permission. I demanded she erase it, because I never gave her permission to take a photo of me. I want it deleted." She crossed her arms, ready to really dig in.

Maybe Harold knew, as he stepped away and then jabbed his hand quite forcefully in the air toward her. "You stay there," he said. Then he walked over to Marcus.

The blonde, who was spitting mad, was still giving Marcus the gears, and she glanced her way with a snarl, the same one she was sending right back.

"I can't believe you tackled that woman."

It was Nathan Rand's sister, wearing a gray wool hat and the same dark coat as yesterday.

"She had it coming," Suzanne said, though she wanted to take it back the minute it was out of her mouth, hearing Harold in her head. *Just stop, already.*

"So why did you do it?" the woman said. "I mean, I heard you defending my brother. You don't know him. This isn't your business."

She didn't miss the confusion staring back at her from dark eyes. Just yesterday, she had been ready to have a go with her, too. "Because it wasn't fair, what happened to your brother," she said, though, from the way the woman was staring at her, maybe she didn't believe her. "Suzanne O'Connell is my name. I guess you should know."

"Mary Carter." The woman pulled off her glove and held out her hand, and Suzanne shook it.

"My boyfriend there is a deputy," Suzanne said. "I made him check the details of your brother's case after what you said. It was statutory rape, and his girlfriend never came forward to clear the air?"

Apparently, she couldn't listen to Harold and drop it.

"Not a word from her," Mary said. "When it went down, I knew it was bad. I told Nathan to watch himself before it happened, but he didn't listen. He said she wasn't like that. When she got pregnant, she didn't have the backbone to stand up to her parents. Her name was Bobbie Weaver. When her father went after Nathan, he was scared, but I don't think he ever believed he'd go that far. More likely, he thought he'd find himself with a beatdown or a bullet in the head. Then the charges came.

"I think it wasn't until he'd been in prison for six months without hearing from Bobbie that it finally sank in. She'd never come clean. Because of where we lived, it had been that easy for him to be charged, tried, and convicted. The Weavers told a story, and they had credibility. I left right after, moved out here, got married. After all the trouble he had out of jail, I convinced Nathan that moving here, he'd be okay, because it wasn't Indiana. Apparently, I was wrong."

The way Mary told her brother's story stirred that outrage inside Suzanne again. No wonder Mary had been so angry the day before. She took in Harold, who was now walking back her way. She'd seen that expression on his face a few times, and on Marcus's too. Just looking at the face of the blonde behind them, she could feel her hand already fisting.

"You get her to erase my photo?"

Harold's expression was grim at her demand. "She

won't show us her phone. She's already called her lawyer, too." He slid his arm out to move Suzanne over, but she didn't. "Look, if she posts it somewhere, we'll go after her, but the lawyer will tell us to get a warrant. Jesus, Suzanne, you tackled her! There are witnesses here. We need you to apologize to her."

She heard Mary chuckle under her breath.

"Fuck off!" she snapped. It just came out. There was no way she'd ever apologize to someone like that.

Harold shut his eyes and shook his head. His lips firmed. There were a lot of things about Harold she loved, and his self-control in situations like this was one of them, but for a moment, he seemed as though he would reach out and shake her.

"I'm not messing around here, Suzanne," he said. "De-escalation is the only option. This isn't the time for this stubbornness of yours, right and wrong, because you can't go around tackling people just because they make you angry. You need to swallow it. You need to listen to me on this! Apologize to her, and then we walk away."

"What, and she gets to keep going around, putting those flyers up, stirring up anger and hate until a mob shows up on Mary's doorstep?" She gestured to Mary, who was staring at her as if she'd lost her mind. Maybe she had, but there was so much wrong with the story she'd heard that it had somehow found a way under her skin, and now there was no way she could do what Harold asked.

"She has every right to notify residents. She's already been warned that she can't post the flyers on post boxes or city utility poles or she'll be fined, but that's all we can do. Apologize!" His voice was low, direct, and she didn't miss the bite of anger.

She just stared at him and then over to Mary. The way she looked at her, Suzanne could see that Rand's sister expected her to cave in, do her boyfriend's bidding, but that would mean having no backbone, and that was something Suzanne couldn't live with. There was right, and there was wrong and lying and cheating, and she'd been on the receiving end of the latter too many times, more than she was comfortable with.

"No." She crossed her arms.

Marcus approached, and there was the blonde. Just looking at her now, she didn't want to tackle her; she wanted to punch her in the face. "Angela has agreed to let this go, Suzanne, if you apologize and help her get the word out."

She dragged her gaze from Marcus back to Harold, who was still looking at her, hard, unbending, willing her to just fall in line. She didn't have to look over to Mary to know that she expected her to do just that.

She dragged her gaze back over to Angela, who wore an expectant expression, looking down on her as if she were someone of more importance. "Let me get this straight," she said to her. "You want me to apologize to you and then help put up flyers about a young man who was fucked around, given a label over something you have the facts all wrong about?"

"You know what?" Angela said. "You're wasting my time. That's not an apology. I want her arrested now, or I'll have your badge and will bring a world of trouble down on you, Sheriff, and your office." She could see this woman was really pushing Marcus's buttons.

"Suzanne, apologize now!" Marcus demanded.

She could see the trouble this woman could cause and get away with. She took in Harold, Mary, and Marcus, then let her gaze linger on Angela, who she figured saw only her own perspective on everything. "You want me to apologize for tackling you? Okay, I'm sorry—because I wish I would've punched you in the face instead. I'll go to jail before helping you defame someone and destroy a life like you are!"

Angela shrieked.

She heard Harold swear under his breath, whereas Marcus had his hands up, trying to calm the outraged woman.

Suzanne held her arms out in front of her. "Arrest me, because I have no intention of apologizing to this bitch."

She didn't think she'd ever forget the shock on Harold and Marcus's faces.

"I demand right now that you arrest her," Angela screamed, "or my lawyer will have your badge!"

There were witnesses standing around, phones recording.

"What are you doing?" Mary said to her, shocked. "Just tell that bitch you're sorry."

She hadn't expected that. She shook her head, feeling cuffs slapped on her wrists. Harold took her arm, pulling her away, and she looked back at Mary and shook her head.

"No, because there's right and wrong, Mary, and someone here has to be willing to stand up and do the right thing."

The back door of Harold's cop car was open, and he put her inside and closed it. She watched him walk around, realizing he'd just arrested her.

Outside, her brother was dealing with Angela. Something about everything that had just happened was telling her she'd gone too far yet again.

Harold slid behind the wheel, started the car, and lifted his gaze to her, then shook his head. "What the hell, Suzanne? All you had to do was apologize."

As he pulled away from the curb, what he was saying hit her, and she shook her head. "You know what? I'm pretty sure you didn't read me my rights. Either way, there's no way you can ever make me say sorry to that bitch."

Harold turned left at the end of the block, into traffic. She couldn't help wondering where this put them, exactly, their relationship. Maybe this would be the final straw for him.

For a second, she had to turn her head to the window, away from the mesh bars that separated him from her. She was hit by a wave of sadness and tears that seemed to come out of nowhere and burned her eyes. All this confusion, uncertainty, and restlessness that had been growing inside her as of late seemed to be spiraling, and now she was in a place she'd never imagined she'd be.

She reached up with her cuffed hands to wipe a tear that spilled down her cheek, staring at the cars driving by, the people who were looking right at her in the back seat as if she were a common criminal. It was a horrible feeling.

She was the master of her own downfall. But right was right, and wrong was wrong, and there was no way she was about to take the easy way out and apologize to a woman who felt she was entitled to one, who had demanded it and looked down on her the way she had, as if Suzanne were less than her.

She wondered, as she stared out the side window, riding in silence, if this was how Nathan Rand had felt when he'd been arrested and then charged. But it had been worse for him, since he now carried a label that would never allow him to live in peace, never have a civilized moment, never live with dignity. He would have to look over his shoulder every day.

Eight

"I thought you would be gone already," Tessa said as she strode into the kitchen, showered, dressed in blue jeans and a light brown sweater over another of his faded blue T-shirts, one he didn't remember seeing in his drawer.

He lifted his mug of coffee and took a swallow. "Nope. Got a text from the owner saying he finished up the job himself last night. Basically told me not to come back."

He knew the owner had likely gone with the band-aid approach instead of letting him finish replacing the busted lines, fixing it right. He'd likely taped them up because he couldn't pay Owen the money. It made Owen sick to think the tenants in that house were the ones getting screwed.

He still needed to go back and pick up the few supplies he'd left to finish the job that day, and he would check in with the family. At least he'd fixed enough the day before that they had running water again—for now.

Tessa only nodded.

He reached for one of the clean mugs beside the coffeemaker and poured her a coffee, then held it out to her. She hesitated for a moment, her blue eyes flicking up to him, and he took in her long blond hair, hanging loose and straight. Evidently, she'd taken the time to dry it instead of sporting the natural waves and frizz that happened when she didn't.

"You heading out somewhere?" he said.

Her fingers touched his as she took the mug, and she shrugged. "At some point. I have a few errands to run, Christmas gifts still to buy, considering shopping with Suzanne yesterday didn't happen."

Right. He needed to check in with his sister. "How about I tag along?"

There it was, that smile he loved, that smile he wanted to wake up to for a lifetime. "You, shopping? I'd pay money to see that."

He knew he made a face, as she gave a soft laugh. "What? I can shop. I may have a few things I need to buy, as well."

He just didn't want to go into every store and look and linger, but then, if she smiled like this, he'd make the sacrifice and find the chair every shop set out for guys like him.

His cell phone was ringing, and he saw it was Marcus. "Wonder what he wants," he said as he reached for it. Tessa seemed relaxed. "Hey. What's up?"

"We have a problem," Marcus said.

That heavy knot in his chest, which he hadn't felt in a while, returned.

"Am I going to want to hear it?" he said, letting his gaze linger on Tessa, who hadn't moved and didn't pull her gaze from him. She leaned against the counter, so close to him.

"Likely not, but you need to get down here to the station and talk some sense into our bullheaded sister. She basically has assault charges pending against her. I had managed to soothe over the woman in question and convince her to drop it, and all Suzanne had to do was apologize—"

He had to tell himself to breathe. "Assault! Excuse me, is she under arrest? Let me guess: She refused to apologize. What did she do? Who did she assault?"

He wasn't sure Tessa's widened eyes could get any bigger. She gestured to him and mouthed, "Who?"

He let the phone slip from his mouth. "Suzanne."

Tessa's mouth gaped a bit, and he heard a squeak. Apparently, she didn't know what to say, either.

"It has to do with Nathan Rand, the flyers," Marcus said. "Apparently, she met the woman who was tacking them up and decided to go down and have a word with her. From there, it didn't go well. It ended up in a heated confrontation, and Suzanne tackled her. There's more, but do you really need me to go into it? She's not listening to me, and Harold…I've never seen him lose composure, but he came pretty close, I'm sure, to wanting to strangle her. She's not listening to him at all. I can hold her for only so long without charging her—which isn't going to happen, if you understand. The problem, though, is that the woman she went after has a high-priced attorney who's on his way down to make sure she's charged or my head's on a platter. And did I add the part about witnesses?"

"On my way," Owen said, then hung up, letting out a sigh.

Tessa was already striding to the door, where she pulled her coat on and slipped on her boots.

"I have to go down to the jail. Suzanne…" he started.

Tessa reached for his coat from the closet and held it out to him. "I know. I heard enough. Let's go."

He took the coat and slipped it on. "You didn't ask for details," he said. He quickly filled Tessa in on what Marcus had told him, then said, "I feel as if I'm having to go down to the principal's office because my little sister gave someone a bloody nose. She did that, you know."

The memory came out of nowhere, and so did the laugh that bubbled up, likely from the shock of this situation they found themselves in. Tessa touched her head and groaned as he slid on his boots, and he reached for her car keys and took them from her. She didn't argue.

"Good God, Owen—and Harold can't get through to her?"

He followed her to her light blue compact, where she pulled open the passenger door. He wondered whether she understood what she was saying, considering he couldn't get through to her, his partner, either.

"Suzanne has a stubborn streak, and apparently Harold has just found himself on the wrong side of it. He can't reason with her. If Marcus is calling me, this is serious. There's one thing I know about Suzanne: When she gets an idea in her head or digs her heels in, you'd have a better chance of moving a mountain. So, again, fill me in on yesterday. Something about her seemed off last night in a way I haven't seen before."

The drive to the station took less than ten minutes,

and he pulled in beside his brother's ranger's pickup. Apparently, Ryan was there as well.

He wasn't sure he was any clearer on what was going on with his sister now than before. Tessa had told him Suzanne wasn't feeling a hundred percent the day before and had been moodier than usual, and she seemed to have way too much time on her hands. As he listened to Tessa talk about his sister, he figured not working was beginning to have an effect on Suzanne and was bringing out this erratic behavior.

"You haven't said two words," Tessa said. "Do you know what you're going to say to her?"

Owen walked up the stairs to the sheriff's office, side by side with Tessa, feeling the tightness in his chest that had been there for what seemed like forever, being the eldest and always having to yank one of his siblings from trouble.

"Nope." He shook his head.

He could hear voices through the door to the sheriff's office, arguing, loud. This was turning into a shitshow, out of control. He exchanged a look with Tessa, who went first through the door, and he spotted a blonde with a man he'd never seen before. Marcus had a look on his face that told Owen he was going to snap. Ryan was talking with Colby, the other deputy, off to the side.

"Excuse me a second," was all Marcus said, then nodded to Owen, who strode around the couple with Tessa. "Colby, show Angela and her lawyer to my office."

Owen followed Marcus through a door down the hall in back where the jail cells were. "What the hell is going on here?" he said. He knew Ryan was there too, walking behind him, and Tessa. He took in the empty cells and heard a voice: Harold, and did he ever sound angry.

Marcus led them down to the last cell. "All manner of hell, and my negotiating skills are wearing thin," was all he said.

They stopped at the open door to the cell, where Suzanne was sitting on a bench, and there was Harold standing over her, his hands on his duty belt. Owen couldn't remember ever seeing him so angry.

"Deal with her," Marcus said, gesturing to him. "Talk some sense into her before there's a three-ring circus outside my station." He glanced in the cell to Suzanne and then shook his head in frustration, not something Owen saw often in his brother.

He gripped the bar of the cell and slid his gaze over to Ryan, who rested his hands on the bars on the other side of the open door. He wasn't sure what to make of Tessa's expression as she stepped inside the cell, taking in the concrete, the toilet in the corner, and the hard bench Suzanne was sitting on.

"I can't talk to her right now," Harold said. "Get through to her that this isn't a joke." He went to step out of the cell before turning back to Suzanne and Tessa, who was now sitting beside her on the hard bench, her arm around her shoulders. "I'll get you some water, something to eat." He gestured down to her, and Owen didn't miss the edge in his voice. Yeah, Harold cared, and his sister had completely cornered him.

She flicked her gaze up and over to him, and he didn't think she'd answer Harold. So she'd gone mute now. Okay, he could understand why Harold looked as if he wanted to kill her.

"That'd be a great idea, Harold," Tessa said for Suzanne.

Owen took in Harold's face as he stepped past him and Ryan, the kind of expression that told him he'd been going up against Suzanne's rock-hard stubbornness.

"So what is this?" Ryan said, stepping into the cell and leaning against the concrete wall. "Your new home?"

"You think I want to be here?"

"Then why are you here, Suzanne?" Owen jumped in. He glanced back to Harold, who was still standing there, shaking his head.

"Because Harold arrested me. He put cuffs on me. You handcuffed me and stuck me in the back of the car like a common criminal and drove me here. People saw me. It was humiliating…"

"Oh, stop it!" Harold snapped. "I took the cuffs off you when I pulled up here. You left me no choice at the scene. Remember standing there, demanding I arrest you, holding your hands up to cuff you? Do you realize there were witnesses? You refused to apologize, which would have made this all go away. It was to make a point, Suzanne. You're not under arrest."

"You handcuffed my sister and put her in the back of your car?" Owen said, turning to Harold, who stared back at him as if ready to have it out.

"She created an untenable situation," Harold said, "a scene that could be controlled only by getting her out of there before she made it any worse. She assaulted a woman by tackling her. There were witnesses, two men, who had to pull her off the woman, who, by the way, is here with her lawyer, demanding Suzanne be brought up on charges of assault, even though Marcus had convinced her to settle for an apology."

"I'm not apologizing to that bitch," Suzanne said. "I tried to explain to her how she had it wrong about Nathan Rand, but she's determined to head up a witch hunt he doesn't deserve. It wasn't just an apology. There was an expectation that I would help her put up flyers. It was a way to tell me I would do what she said, or else. That wasn't lost on me. It's kind of what happened to Nathan Rand, don't you think?"

"You didn't have to say you wished you'd put your fist in her face. You tossed gasoline on a fire we had almost managed to put out."

"So she wanted Suzanne to put up flyers and help, and you went along with this," Ryan said, gesturing to Harold. He sounded unusually calm. Suzanne was nodding as if someone was on her side.

"She wants us to press charges," Harold said. "The fact is that Suzanne assaulted her. She demanded an apology and for Suzanne to help her put up flyers. Marcus already set her straight on where she can and can't post them—"

"But you didn't ticket her for posting flyers on city property and mailboxes. You just let her go," Suzanne said.

"We gave her a warning, which is what we wanted to do for you. What do you expect, Suzanne, a three-ring circus? You want her ticketed with a fine and you charged with assault? No! I can't believe this. Just apologize!"

"I'm not putting up flyers," Suzanne said. "It's defamation, what she's doing to Nathan and his sister. Did you know he got his girlfriend pregnant? That's what this was about. She was seventeen, and she never made a statement or came forward. It was entirely the father, the sheriff, the small Indiana town. Mary, Nathan's sister, was there today. I spoke with her, and she told me her brother waited for his girlfriend to do the right thing. He believed she would until he was six months into his jail term and she still hadn't come forward. How could she do that to him?"

Owen found himself looking back at Harold, who shrugged.

"Look, it still happens in places, that 1950s justice," Harold said. "I didn't say it was fair. It doesn't happen here, Suzanne. Unfortunately, I can't change what happened to Mr. Rand. You know your brother doesn't do things that way here, but I can't fix the problems happening elsewhere in this country. I empathize, I really do—but, Suzanne, this is about you. The only situation we're dealing with is this one. We need this to go away, with no charges against you. You can't go around assaulting people." Harold dragged his gaze over to Owen. "Please get through to her." Then Harold pushed away from the cell and walked out.

Owen waited for the door at the end of the hall to close, then gazed back down to his sister. "So what's really going on, Suzanne? You and Harold having problems? You haven't worked in some time. Why don't you come and help me and Brady out? I could always use more hands, and you're pretty good with yours."

She was shaking her head. "I'm not going to be another apprentice you can tell what to do, making me carry your tools around. I'm not a plumber. I can find my own job, thank you very much. Anyway, this is about someone who didn't get a fair shake. You know, when this was going on, that crazy bitch, Angela, looked down on me as if she was better than me, as if she could do whatever she wanted and didn't care what anyone thought. Mary expected me to just give in and cower, to fall in line with Angela's demands. I saw her face. She thought I wasn't going to stand up for what I believe in. Can you imagine someone doing that? When have I ever allowed someone to tell me how to think, what to feel, or sacrificed my beliefs?"

He just stared at his sister, seeing the passion there. He knew she was right, but he didn't know how to make her understand. "I get it, Suzanne. I really do. But you can't be a schoolyard bully, giving someone a bloody nose because you don't like what she says or does. You call the police. You let Harold and Marcus deal with her. You're not a cop—"

"Well, maybe I should be," she said.

He wasn't sure if the shock on Ryan's face matched his. He'd have paid real money to see Marcus's expression in response to that.

"You'd make a fine cop, Suzanne," Tessa said.

"You think so?" Suzanne said. There she was, reasonable again.

"Of course you would," Tessa said. "Look at you. But I don't think you can be a cop if you have a record…"

Owen really looked at her, seeing the way she was so supportive of his sister and seemed to be talking her language.

"I'm not putting up flyers," Suzanne said, her stubbornness back.

"Nor should you have to." Tessa lifted her gaze to Owen as if he could figure out a way to fix this. "But, as

I tell my students, you can't get physical with someone because she made you angry or did something you don't like. You have to apologize to her for that. Come on, Suzanne. You can do it."

The way Tessa was talking to her, reasonable, he could see his sister starting to come around.

"I would rather chew on nails than say I'm sorry," Suzanne said.

Tessa rubbed her shoulder. "Oh, I can imagine, and I completely get it. But do it. Dig deep. I know that you, Suzanne, who went toe to toe with a bully and didn't cower, didn't bend on her ideals and beliefs for anyone, can find a way to apologize. About the flyer thing, Owen, you go and talk to Harold and Marcus, because there's no way she's putting any up."

Three pairs of eyes were looking his way expectantly, as if the outcome were entirely up to him.

"I'll do what I can," was all he said.

He strode away, hearing Tessa and Suzanne talking. As he reached the door, he realized that as difficult as Suzanne was, he may have a bigger obstacle to deal with on the other side, this Angela and her lawyer. Then there were Marcus and Harold. He didn't know why, but it seemed he was stepping into it once again, fixing something in his family. It wasn't lost on him that everyone still looked to him as if he could fix anything.

He wondered if there would ever come a point that he'd let one of them down.

O wen stepped out of the back and pulled the door closed behind him, taking in Colby on the phone, standing at his desk. The expression on his face was one he hadn't seen before. There were other lines ringing, and he spotted Therese, her dark hair cut short, her head down, in her deputy uniform. Marcus's door was closed, yet he could hear the voices from behind it, angry, upset, outraged.

"The phone has been ringing nonstop about the sheriff's sister," Colby said. "Apparently, word is out, and accusations are being called in. Every one of these calls is about us fixing a charge because she's his sister." Colby was agitated as he held the phone and then pressed another line, saying, "Sheriff's office."

He could hear Therese on the phone, too, and it sounded as if she was dealing with the same thing. He only reached over and patted Colby's arm, because what could he say?

Just then, the front door opened, and there were his mom, Luke, and his good old dad. He didn't know why, but seeing Raymond O'Connell here set him on edge in a way he couldn't have explained. He jammed his hands in his coat pockets and stood there as his mom approached first, Luke and their dad behind her.

"Where is she?" Iris demanded.

He tilted his head to the door. "Back there. Tessa and Ryan are with her."

"I swear, Harold has gone too far…"

"Mom, you can't put this on Harold. You know Suzanne. She put them in an untenable situation. She isn't arrested or charged yet, but they've parked her ass there so she'll see reason—and she has, for the most part, with Tessa's encouragement."

His mom had her own stubborn streak, he knew. She dragged her gaze over to the door, to the cell in back.

"You should go back there," he said.

She nodded only once before doing so. Then Luke and his dad were right there, in his face.

"So fill me in. She really tackled this lady?" Luke said, his expression amused.

"I'm sure one day we'll all laugh about this, but yes, she really did. Quite the cat fight. I presume you're up to speed. Right now, she's agreed to apologize, but that's it. The lady in question right now is in with Marcus."

The front door opened again, and there was Harold, his coat on, carrying a bottle of water and a wrapped sandwich. He walked straight over to them. "You're out here, so please tell me she's now seeing the light of day."

"She's agreed to apologize," Owen said. "That's it. That's the only concession—and, frankly, I agree with her. She won't help that woman make Nathan Rand's life more difficult or join the witch hunt. I can't believe

Marcus would go along with that, or you. You did look into his case, right? There isn't something more glaring, like he really is genuinely, legitimately a predator and should be on that registry? Because I hate to tell you, but Suzanne seems to have dug her heels in. She does live and die by her principles and isn't going to let this slide. Also, you should know she's also talking about becoming a cop."

He wasn't sure for a moment whether Harold was going to respond. He stilled, and his expression wasn't amused. Then he nodded. It seemed he needed to take a second to try to wrap his head around this.

"I'm going to take this back," he finally said. "I know she didn't eat, and…" He tilted his head to Marcus's closed door, the muffled voices that sounded like demands.

"Yeah, go. I got this," Owen said.

As Harold opened the door to the cells in back, Owen went to take a step to Marcus's office.

"Hang on a second, Owen," Raymond said. "Let's take a minute here. You know anything about the woman in there, her lawyer? Because if we're trying to de-escalate the situation, it sounds like walking in and saying please isn't going to cut it."

Just something about the way his dad said it made Owen feel like Raymond somehow believed he was in charge here.

"You think I don't know that?" Owen said. "Believe me, this is my sister—"

"And my daughter," Raymond shot right back in a low voice, then glanced back to Colby, who was at Therese's desk, out of hearing range.

"Don't walk in here and think you can play dad and

fix things, because you can't," Owen said. "I've been pulling everyone out of a jam since the day you left. You don't get to walk in now. Suzanne is my little sister. Every jam she's gotten into, I've been the one there for her, not you."

He knew it had come out rather sharply, and he didn't miss the sharp shush from Luke. He found himself lifting his hands in surrender, taking a step back. Luke angled his head to him as he stepped closer.

"I'm not stepping on toes here, Owen," Raymond said. "I'm well aware of everything you've done and had to do, but having a pissing contest now over who gets priority isn't going to help this situation or make it go away. Time is not on Suzanne's side. This is escalating. All I'm suggesting is having the facts first. We don't know this woman's agenda or the reasons she did what she did, why she's so angry, why she's here with a lawyer, demanding something that seems unreasonable to you. Again, this is about knowing the details of what you're dealing with first. Let's find out what she really wants."

"He's right," Luke said in a low voice. "We need to do it before this dog and pony show turns into the community demanding Suzanne's head on a spike. A spin is happening. You can see it, hear it. I can feel we're in it already. I know how it's going to go. I've seen this kind of thing happen too many times. We're going down a slippery slope, fast picking up speed. I'll be damned if Suzanne's going to have to go down for this, so listen to what he's saying." Luke settled his hand on Owen's shoulder, and something passed between them.

Owen had to force himself to look over to his dad. "Fair enough. As you can see, Suzanne's in back now.

The woman in question is in there with her lawyer and Marcus."

"I already made a call," Luke cut in.

Owen knew what that meant. His brother had called someone that normal people didn't deal with, someone way above his clearance.

Marcus's office door opened, and he took in his brother's unsmiling face. The short, dark-haired lawyer in a long black coat was still talking behind him with Angela.

Just then, the door to the cells opened, and there was Ryan.

"Call an ambulance!" he shouted. "Suzanne fainted or something. She just fell over—"

Luke had his phone out, and Marcus hurried past them to the cell door. Meanwhile, Owen watched as his dad walked over to the lawyer and the woman, who had suddenly fallen quiet.

Owen was torn on what to do: go back to his sister or handle the problem, which it seemed Raymond O'Connell was determined to do?

"Ambulance is coming," Luke said.

Owen went to take a step, looking over to their dad, but Luke rested a hand on his shoulder again.

"He's got this," he said. "This is what he does, Owen. We all have something we're good at. Our only objective is Suzanne, here."

Owen just found himself taking in his brother, wondering why Luke found it so easy to let things go with their dad. "I don't understand why you're so willing to give him a pass."

Luke let out a sigh and pulled his hand away. It was just them at the back of the sheriff's office. Whatever their dad was saying, he'd have given anything to be over there, hearing it. "I'm not giving anyone a pass, but maybe I understand what he did because I was fortunate enough to not have the same fate. I know what he chose to do. Now, go back and check on Suzanne."

From the way Luke's gaze lingered, Owen realized it.

"Do I want to know what you two are going to do?" he said.

There it was, that odd smile, a flicker of something. Luke tapped his shoulder again. "Go," was all he said, and Owen knew he had his answer. Luke strode over to the lady, the lawyer, and their dad.

Hearing a commotion on the stairs, Owen turned to see the door opening as two paramedics stepped inside.

Marcus appeared from the back, gesturing for them. "She's back here," he called out before stepping over to Owen. "She's awake. Swears it's low blood sugar since she didn't eat." He jutted his chin toward Luke and their dad. "Am I going to want to know what that's about?"

All Owen did was settle his hand on Marcus's shoulder as he said, "Probably not."

CHAPTER

Ten

Suzanne pulled off her oxygen mask as she took in the curtain in the emergency room. She was still on the bed, in her sweats, and Harold was standing right there.

"Leave it on," he said, moving to put it back on her, but she shook her head.

"I'm fine. I don't need it, Harold, please. This is embarrassing, having two paramedics I used to work with taking me to the hospital from the jail. If word wasn't out about me before, it is now. I didn't eat, is all…"

"You fainted," he snapped. "You keeled over where you were sitting, right on Tessa. What do they call it, a syncopal episode? First you were dizzy yesterday and almost fell over, and now this? This is more than not eating. So lie down, stay put, and please, for once, just listen to me."

She could see that his patience had left, and Harold could take a lot until he wouldn't be pushed anymore. "Look, I've been poked and prodded, my blood taken, tests ordered. I guarantee you I'm fine. I don't need this." She put the oxygen mask aside even though, and she'd never admit it, there had been a moment when they brought her in on the stretcher, lightheaded, that she'd needed it. "I want to go home," she said. And then she'd have to apologize. "Or do you need to take me back to jail?"

He actually dropped the F-bomb under his breath just as the curtain flicked aside, and Suzanne took in the doctor, a young woman with dark round cheeks and a smile, wearing scrubs.

"I'm Doctor Jones," she said. "Your tests just came back, and I think we need to have a conversation here—in private, if you don't mind, Deputy. I'll ask you to step out…"

"I do mind," Harold said. "I'm not leaving. Suzanne is my partner, although, some days, it doesn't seem like it. What's wrong with her? What did the tests show?" He was quite short with the doctor, whose expression was guarded, and Suzanne had the horrible sinking feeling that it was bad news.

"What is it?" she said. "Is something wrong?"

"No, no, nothing like that," Doctor Jones said. "Don't go thinking the worst. Is it okay…?" She gestured to Harold, not wanting to say anything out of turn.

"Yes, it's fine," Suzanne said. "As he said, we live together." She glanced to him. "I love him."

He lifted his hand and pressed it to her forehead, brushing back her hair.

"Well, okay then," the doctor said. "We ran some tests, and it came back that you're slightly anemic—and pregnant."

That last bit had her staring at the doctor.

"Pregnant," Harold said.

Suzanne just stared, trying to figure out how she hadn't known. Wasn't being pregnant something women just knew? Maybe that was why her clothes weren't fitting, why she'd felt so off.

"Would that by any chance bring on erratic behavior?" Harold crossed his arms, standing right beside the bed, giving everything to the doctor in that all-cop way of his.

"Well, big hormonal spikes and changes in the body do cause some personality changes, yes , and mood swings," the doctor said. "Is there something concerning that you're talking about?" She had a stethoscope around her neck, and there was still a blood pressure cuff draped over her arm. She pulled a penlight from her shirt pocket and flicked it on. "Suzanne, look up here." She shone it in her eyes.

"Oh, just fighting, arguing, not seeing reason..." Harold said.

Suzanne wanted to look away, but the doctor pressed her hand to her head, looking in her eyes. When she flicked the light off, shaking her head, Suzanne wasn't sure if she smiled in amusement or in a way that said she'd heard this kind of thing before.

"Don't listen to him," Suzanne said. "I was just standing up for something that was right...and I may have tackled someone."

"Okay, I'm going to stop you right there," the doctor said. "No more fighting. No hand-to-hand combat or whatever it is you're doing. You're pregnant. I asked someone from OB to come down so they can do an ultrasound to see how far along you are. But the anemia part is concerning. Your iron levels are too low, so you'll need to take vitamins and eat better, eat more iron-rich foods. Your OB will talk to you about that. Take a breath, both of you. This is good news."

The doctor hesitated, taking them both in, before shaking her head. What she was thinking, Suzanne didn't have a clue. She knew the paramedics had already announced that she was from the jail.

When the doctor stepped out of the curtained-off area, Harold pressed his hand to the bed and looked down at her. The growing anger and frustration that had been in his expression moments earlier had changed. He really was handsome, even though he didn't have the pretty-boy features some men did, or the kind of charisma that oozed. He had such hard, chiseled features, and she didn't even notice the scars on his face anymore. They just added to the man she loved more than anything. The way he looked at her with those hazel eyes, all she could think was that she was pregnant with his baby.

"Well, I guess I have an idea now why you've been so off," he said. "I have to wonder if this is what I'm in for the entire time you're pregnant. I may have to lock you in the condo for the day so you can't leave and stir up any more trouble."

She actually rolled her eyes as he rested his hand on her shoulder, her arm. He seemed to know she wanted to sit up, as he lifted the back of the gurney.

"I'm sorry, but I'm not helping her put up flyers," she said.

He reached over and let the back of his fingers run over her cheek, and he nodded. "I know you're not, but I'm also tired of having to cuff members of this family.

You have no idea, but this doesn't sit well with me. You go head to head with people sometimes, Suzanne, so much like a pit bull, not backing down. You think nothing of putting my back to the wall, anyone's, and sometimes it's right, but sometimes you have to tell yourself, now's not the time. How about you promise that if you're about to do something crazy, you call me first?"

"I want to be a cop," she said. She couldn't stop herself. She took in how he stilled. "I would make a great cop, a great addition to the department here."

"How about we focus on you and this baby right now?" Harold cut in. She wasn't sure whether he was about to tell her no. "And we'll talk about that at a much later date."

She knew what he was doing. "I want to feel important and do something meaningful and make a difference."

The sigh he let out sounded more like a groan. "You're going to be the end of me." He scowled.

"But you love me, right?" she said.

He ran his hand over her leg and leaned in, then pressed a kiss to her lips and let it linger. It was soft, caring. She lifted her hand and touched his cheek, and he pulled back just a bit, so close to her.

"Marry me," he said in a low voice, and for a moment, she wasn't sure she'd heard him right.

"Is it because I'm pregnant?" she said. Of course, she needed to know, but the edge in his expression told her he'd taken it the wrong way.

"I asked you because I love you, with all your faults and moods, even when I never know who I'm going to find waiting for me at home—even though there's never a dull moment with you, even though there are days like today where I want to pull my hair out because I can't reason with you. You're difficult and stubborn, but I've never met someone who will stand up for what she believes in the way you do. You being pregnant has only bumped up what I already wanted to do. You haven't answered me, Suzanne. This is it, no hearts and flowers, but if you want that, I'll get it for you."

It was just the way he said it, just the way he touched her, the way his hand ran over hers and linked with it.

"Okay," she said.

"Yes?" he prompted.

She shrugged. "Yeah, I'll marry you, but there's still the matter of the pending charges against me."

Harold shook his head. His hand squeezed hers. "No, there won't be. Don't worry about. You will have to apologize to her as soon as Marcus smooths it over. You think I don't know how you feel? I do. I know how it feels to have to swallow something because you're forced to even though it goes against everything you believe in. Pick your battles, Suzanne. I've worked for assholes over the years who got off on grinding me into the ground. You think there haven't been times that I wanted to fight them or refuse? I get it. I do."

The way he said it, the way he really looked at her with those hazel eyes, she knew she loved much more about this man than his ability to control his feelings so much better than she could.

"Okay, just tell me where and when," she said.

He didn't nod as he reached over and tucked her hair behind her ears. Just then, the curtain was brushed back, and another doctor appeared with an ultrasound.

"So you're having a baby," she said, pushing in the

machine. "Let's find out how far along you are. Are you ready to see?"

Suzanne looked over to Harold and held out her hand. "Yeah, and I want a photo to show my family, to put on the fridge."

Harold only nodded as the doctor lowered the bed, lifted her gown, squirted jelly on her belly, and settled the wand there.

There it was, her baby.

The heartbeat echoed.

And this, suddenly, became oh so real.

CHAPTER
Eleven

Owen pulled into Marcus's driveway and parked behind Charlotte's Subaru, leaving the car in gear as he turned off the engine. Tessa reached over and touched his arm as he pulled the key from the ignition.

"Just hold up a second," she said. "I want to talk to you. Can we just sit here a second? I feel today has kind of gone off the deep end with everything that happened, Suzanne, the jail, that woman, Suzanne going to the hospital… No one has heard anything yet."

He knew what she was talking about. He was still shaken over seeing his sister really dig into something that could seriously jam her up. "Sure, whatever you need," he said, then reached over and took Tessa's hand, taking in her long slim fingers, her bomber jacket. She looked straight ahead, and he could feel something as he held her hand. "What is it?"

She pulled in a breath, then dragged her gaze over to him. She didn't smile. "Do you think your sister is okay?"

He was still having a hard time shaking his worry at seeing Suzanne on a stretcher, being taken out of the jail. "I'm sure she is." He hoped she was. "Maybe someone has already heard."

She only nodded. "You know, yesterday, Suzanne really scared me, confronting that woman. She wasn't scared at all. Then, today, seeing the way she was standing up for her principles and fighting for someone she still doesn't know… She was ready to fall on her sword. I've never seen your sister so sure about something, I mean, she was so strong in her belief. I guess a piece of me really envies the fact that she went into something that would've scared anyone else into backing down, but not her."

He was still holding Tessa's hand. The snow was starting to fall, and the cold outside was making its way into the warm car. "Suzanne has always been stubborn. She often gave the impression of being a sweet kid, but man, if you pissed her off, or if there was something she wanted to do or planned to do or believed in, you couldn't change her mind. When she landed that job at the fire department, I knew she'd found her calling. I know losing that was hard on her."

Tessa leaned back against the seat and looked over to him. There was that smile for him. Her blue eyes softened. "You're the best big brother ever, the way you always have your siblings' backs, no matter what. Just watching you today when I was sitting beside Suzanne in that jail cell, I could see how much you loved her and wanted to strangle her at the same time. You're such a good man, Owen. When I knew you were going to do what you could to sort it out for her, I wanted to race after you and tell you what a fool I've been…"

He wasn't sure he'd heard her right. Her smile disappeared, and there was something so deep and touching in the way her gaze reached out to him.

"I love you so much, Owen, and I know I haven't made this easy for you. I put all my fears about something that seems so silly now into our relationship. But I know that's not you and would never be you. Ask me again."

It took him another second to understand what she was saying.

"You mean when I asked you to marry me?"

She nodded. "Ask me again."

The car was so damn small. He couldn't even turn in his seat as he reached over and touched her cheek. "Tessa, will you marry me?"

She pulled in a breath and flicked her gaze away as if considering, then looked back at him. "I thought you'd never ask," she said. "Yes, I would very much love to marry you, Owen." She reached over and slid her hand over his cheek, touching his hair, and the way she really looked at him, he could see how much she meant it.

"Yes?"

Her smile deepened again, "Yes. Oh, yes, Owen. Even as terrified as I am, I know it's a ridiculous fear. It makes me so mad now to think I could've blown it with you…"

He reached for her hand on his cheek and pressed a kiss into her palm, then leaned over in the small car and kissed her lips, letting it linger.

A sharp knock on his window had him pulling back and opening his door, seeing Ryan and Jenny.

"What the hell are you two doing in there?" Ryan

said, gesturing. "It's cold out here. Come inside."

Tessa stepped out of her side, and he closed the door, seeing his brother with his hand on Jenny's back, walking up the stairs.

"You hear from Harold or Suzanne?" he called out.

Ryan turned back. "Nope, but Marcus may have."

He waited for Tessa, who walked around the front of the vehicle, and he took her hand and followed her up and inside Marcus's house. Ryan pulled off his coat, and so did Jenny. His mom and dad were already there, and so was Luke in the living room.

"We should wait for everyone to get here before we tell them," Owen said.

Marcus strode up, holding Cameron in his arms. "Tell us what?" he said, seeming distracted but still dragging his gaze between Tessa and Owen. "I just got a call from Harold. He and Suzanne are on their way over."

"When they get here, we'll tell everyone," Owen said. "So what about the charges and stuff? With Suzanne heading off to the hospital, where does everything sit? What did Harold say happened to Suzanne? What was wrong?"

Marcus only shook his head. He didn't look happy. "Suzanne has to apologize. The woman is still insisting she help alert the community to a predator. They're calling for community service. Suzanne won't want to hear it. When Harold called, he didn't say what was wrong with Suzanne, but it can't be anything too serious or she'd still be there. We'll find out soon. There they are." He jutted his chin to Harold's Kia pulling up out front. "But, seriously, what is it you want to tell us?"

Owen just reached over to his brother and touched

his shoulder, then shrugged off his coat. "After Suzanne and Harold get here."

"Good news?" He just wouldn't let it go.

"We think so," he said.

Tessa had shrugged out of her coat too, and he reached for her hand as they strode into the living room. He heard voices outside on the steps, and the door opened, and there was his sister, a smile on her face and Harold behind her with a watchful, protective look.

Something was up.

Harold really did have his hands full with Suzanne, he mused.

Tessa was right in front of him where he stood, and he wrapped his arms around her, and she leaned into him. He spotted Brady and Cassie over by the window, too.

"Well, first, before the inquisition starts, Harold and I have some news we want to share," Suzanne said.

Harold had taken her coat and tossed it over the bench with his, still in his uniform and duty belt, not having changed yet. There was something different about him. He didn't seem as ready to strangle his sister as he had been at the jail.

"Please tell me it's not another situation I have to negotiate your way out of," Marcus said.

Suzanne jabbed his stomach and then rubbed Cameron's back. Owen wasn't sure what to make of the expression, the odd smile that touched the edges of Harold's lips.

"Suzanne is pregnant," Harold said. "Almost four months along, believe it or not, and we're getting married."

The room erupted. His mom, Jenny, and even Tessa

raced over to Suzanne, hugging her and giving congratulations, and he found himself shaking his head, suddenly now able to understand what had seemed so off about his sister.

"Tessa and I also have some news," he said, taking in his bride to be, who was standing with Suzanne. "We're also getting married."

He felt his brother slap his back over more congratulations and hugs.

Yet they still had to sort out the problem at the root of all of this.

"We still need to talk about this situation with Suzanne," Marcus said. "Angela and her lawyer are really pushing for assault charges."

Charlotte took Cameron from him. Eva was sitting with his mom now, and Owen could see how she was listening to all of it.

Harold stepped into the room, taking in all of them. "Suzanne has agreed to apologize, but there's no way she's helping this woman put flyers up and let her grind her into the ground. And I agree with her."

Raymond, who had been leaning against the back of the sofa, now stood up straight, taking them all in. "Well then we'll just make sure she accepts the apology," he said.

No one said anything.

Owen looked at a man he still didn't know how to feel about. "And how exactly do you suppose we'll make that happen?" he said.

His father looked right at him when he replied, "By giving her what she really wants."

"I feel absolutely ridiculous," Suzanne said as she rang the doorbell of the two-story house, holding a tray of shortbread cookies that her mom and the other girls had helped her bake. The tray was decorated for Christmas, flashy.

She took in her dad beside her, then glanced back to see Harold and Marcus waiting in the driveway. For a reason she couldn't make sense of, she couldn't shake the nerves that she never allowed herself to have. Then the door opened, and she was looking in the face of a woman she was having a hard time thinking of in a civil way.

They stared at each other with what she thought was the same loathing.

Then she felt Owen nudge her from where he flanked her other side. She forced herself to look up at her big brother, who had always been there for her.

"I made these for you," she said. They're Christmas cookies. Actually, it was my whole family." She held the tray out.

Angela had perfect makeup, the perfect hair, and her outfit seemed both classy and casual, cream and black. She swept her hand back. "Come in. Well, thank you for the cookies."

As Angela reached for the tray and stepped back, Suzanne felt her dad touch the small of her back, so she stepped inside in her bulky winter coat, her hat with a pompom, and her heavy winter boots. Owen stepped in behind her, and her dad closed the door after him. Marcus and Harold were still outside.

"Are they okay waiting outside?" Angela asked.

Her dad looked at the door and shrugged. "They're fine. They're just here for moral support, is all. Jake is my name, and this is Owen, Suzanne's brother." He held out his hand, having used his alias, as always. "Is your husband here as well?"

Angela set the tray down on the table in the entry way. "No, sorry. He's out running errands. Come in. I made coffee and tea."

Suzanne glanced down from taking in the vaulted ceilings. She looked over to Owen, who gave her that expectant look. She needed to get this over with, so she stepped out of her boots and followed the woman into a large open living room with a decorated tree that looked as if it had been pulled from a fashion magazine.

Everything was perfect. She took in the tray with cups. The last thing she wanted was to have to sit and break bread with her.

"I just wanted to say…" Suzanne started.

"That you have a beautiful house," Raymond cut in, then gestured for Suzanne to go and sit on the sofa. "I would love a coffee. Owen?"

She wondered if the breath she pulled in sounded as impatient to everyone as it did to her.

"No, nothing for me," Owen said.

Suzanne found herself sitting on a cream-colored sofa, her bulky jacket still on, Owen beside her. He just shrugged, because her dad was making this painful for her.

Angela poured him a coffee, smiling brightly, and Suzanne took in the silence of the house. The picture above the fireplace was of a toothless little girl. So she had kids.

"Is that your daughter?" Raymond gestured to the photo.

Suzanne wanted to cut in and get to the point, but she hesitated, seeing the way Angela lifted her gaze and wrapped her arms around her chest.

"Tina-Marie, my angel," she said. "She was murdered when she was eight."

For a second, as she dragged her gaze back to the photo and realized it was like a shrine, she felt an intense sorrow that squeezed at her chest.

"What happened to her?" Suzanne asked. Her dad was still standing by the sofa table, watching her.

Angela took a seat with a mug of tea in a wingback chair not far from her. "She was so happy, always smiling. She loved the park. She could spend forever there. I was busy that day. I don't even remember what it was now, some cake I had to make for something. She pleaded with me. It was just at the end of the street, the end of the block, so she'd go herself. I said no, because she was only eight, but her father kept nagging at me to stop being so overprotective, reminding me that at eight, we walked to our friends' houses, went to school ourselves, went to the park with friends… This was a good neighborhood, safe. So, against my better judgement, I let her go."

Suzanne didn't think she could breathe. She wondered whether that was why Owen ran his hand over her shoulder. She nodded.

"She went missing," Raymond said.

Angela nodded in sorrow, pulled into a memory Suzanne didn't want in her head. "She'd been gone not even an hour. I took the cake out of the oven and walked down the street to the park. It was at the end of the block, six houses down. The kids in the neighborhood always went there. But she wasn't there. I asked each of them, and no one had seen her. She had never made it—because a convicted pedophile had moved onto our street, right next to the park."

Owen's hand was still on her shoulder. For a moment, she was horrified at the hate she'd felt for this woman.

"I'm so sorry," Suzanne said. "What happened? …How?"

Her dad appeared far too calm, and she realized he already knew the story.

Angela settled her tea on a small oval table beside her and crossed her legs. Suzanne could see tension. Suddenly, it seemed as if the perfection in how she dressed and held herself was just a mask, the kind of armor one wore to hide her pain.

"She was found in his basement three weeks later, in a trunk. He'd molested her, strangled her…"

"More than twenty years ago now, wasn't it?" Raymond said.

Angela nodded. "It was '93, the year before the sex

offender registry came into effect. He just moved right in. If I'd had any idea…"

Suzanne pressed her hand to her flat stomach, to her baby growing inside. She'd heard its heartbeat and could now feel the flutter. "I am so sorry. So that was why you were so adamant about putting up those flyers."

Angela dragged her gaze over to her, and though she could still see the hardness that had made her want to hate her, she felt like such a fool now. "Yes. If I'd had any idea, my daughter would still be alive. That monster wouldn't have been there in our neighborhood. If someone had just let us know… He wasn't allowed near children. He already had a record. He wasn't allowed to be near a park, but the law didn't protect us then."

"I get it. I really do," Suzanne said. She felt Owen squeeze her shoulder, likely to tell her to stop, but she couldn't. "When I met Mary pulling down those flyers, I felt the same outrage. But Nathan Rand didn't rape anyone. It was his high-school girlfriend. He had just turned eighteen, and she was seventeen, when he got her pregnant. Her father didn't like the fact that he was black, and in that small Indiana town, he didn't have a chance. The father made the police press charges, created a story…"

"Suzanne, Angela doesn't want to hear you defend Nathan Rand," Raymond said.

Angela relaxed a bit and looked to her dad in agreement.

"But, Angela," Raymond continued, "Suzanne is right. The boy was a kid in love, and he'd been dating the girl for two years before he was eighteen. He has a child he'll never be able to see because his girlfriend was too afraid to speak up to her father, and the law would hear only him, not her. He was charged with statutory rape. May I ask how old you were when you started dating your husband?"

She just stared at her dad, wondering what he knew. A lot, it seemed.

Angela shrugged and made a face. "I was sixteen, and my husband was nineteen."

Suzanne wanted to say *See?* But her dad shot her a look from where he stood, warning her not to say anything.

"How old were you when you got married?" he said.

"It's not the same thing."

"No, you're right. It's not. This is Montana, not Indiana, and you and your husband are both white."

Suzanne could see that her dad's words were having the right effect.

"Angela, I'm so sorry for how I reacted," Suzanne said, "for tackling you and yelling at you and not hearing you. You were just trying to protect the kids in the neighborhood. My God, I really get that...but I won't help you with Nathan Rand. He'll be hunted forever. He'll never have any peace. He's not a predator. I won't help you put up flyers to chase him out. If he were a pedophile, I'd be right there with you. But he was just a kid who fell in love with the wrong girl... If you still want to press charges against me, I can't stop you, but I truly am sorry."

Angela lifted her hand. Her gaze was lowered. When she looked right at Suzanne, she could see the lines of sorrow she had evidently tried to hide around her blue eyes. "No, Suzanne, I'm not going to push for charges. I'll call off my lawyer." She stood up. "Well, thank you for the cookies and the apology," she said, trying to force some lightness into her tone. She shook her head. "I guess I should get dinner started for when my husband gets home…"

She started walking, her head high, and Suzanne realized she was seeing an act. She looked over to Owen, who stood beside her and nodded toward the front door.

As they walked there, Angela was fussing with a Christmas arrangement on the entry table. Suzanne stepped into her boots.

"Thanks for the coffee, Angela," Raymond said and held out his hand to shake hers. The smile he offered her was warm.

"You're welcome, Jake," she replied, then pulled in a breath.

Owen pulled open the door, and Suzanne looked back over to Angela—then took one step and then another. She hugged her, feeling her tension and hearing her surprise.

"Merry Christmas, Angela," she said. She stepped back.

Angela seemed unsettled, but she forced a smile to her face. "You too, Suzanne. Merry Christmas."

Then Suzanne stepped out of the house, her dad and Owen beside her, and they started over to Harold and Marcus, who were waiting. Suzanne took in her family, feeling for the first time how lucky she was.

CHAPTER

Thirteen

Christmas with the O'Connells this year was a loud and noisy affair. Instead of Christmas carols playing in the background from the stereo, the football game was on TV, and the mountain of gifts under the Christmas tree had all been opened. Jack and Karen had arrived the day before, meaning everyone was there at his mom's house.

Owen had surprised Tessa that morning with a ring that, to him, matched her personality. Quirky and gorgeous. She'd loved it.

Apparently, Harold had done the same for Suzanne, as she and Tessa had spent the day comparing rings. A girl thing, he thought, as Karen, Jenny, and Charlotte joined in the fussing.

"So all is well," Raymond said from beside him. "I heard Angela reached out to Mary Carter, even went over to meet Nathan Rand."

They were standing just off to the side of the Christmas tree, where Owen could see everyone. Luke had Eva on his back, giving her a piggyback ride into the kitchen, where he could smell the turkey roasting in the oven.

"I didn't know that," Owen said. "That's good news. So how did you know everything? I mean, I never asked you, when we left Angela's, about everything that happened to her. I think back now, and I don't remember about her daughter. I didn't know what to expect when we went to her house, but I'm positive you did."

His dad didn't pull his gaze at first. Then, as if thinking of what to say, he looked away. "There's always a story, a reason someone does something. Often, we don't know what it is, and we see only what's right in front of us, not the reason behind it. I do remember what happened to her girl. You kids were so young, but I remember. What that man did to that little girl should never have happened, but there was no registry then. No one knew someone like that could be living right next door. It was horrible. I don't know what I would've done if that had been one of you. I would've killed him without question."

Owen just nodded. "So you found out all of that about her. When we took Suzanne to apologize, how did you know she wouldn't press charges? Because I didn't. Hearing her story, I felt for her, but there was a moment where I didn't think Suzanne would get a break."

His dad said nothing for a minute. Then he replied, "Her husband's name is Bick McCloskey. He owns a chain of sporting goods stores and has a mistress in the county over, whom he lives with. He never divorced Angela because of what happened. He blamed himself for convincing her to let their daughter walk to the park. He lets her pretend they're still together. He comes by every now and then, but she eats alone, sleeps alone, and pretends her life isn't as miserable as it is. She pretends not to know he lives with another woman."

He just stared in horror, realizing what his dad was saying.

"Luke found out Bick cheated his taxes," Raymond continued. "I convinced the man it was in his best interest to smooth things over with his wife."

Suzanne seemed so radiant now, and it wasn't lost on him that she hadn't stopped smiling all day. Harold was on the sofa with Marcus, each with a beer in his hand and the game on TV. Neither said anything.

"So you already knew how it would go when we walked in there," Owen said.

His dad shrugged. "I did. But I learned long ago how to control a situation. Suzanne didn't understand what had happened to Angela. There's righteous anger, and then there's having empathy for someone who is still grieving. The only thing Angela wanted was to be heard. We listened. Angela is apparently helping Nathan reach out to his child, to the young lady in Indiana. The boy is eight years old now."

"But it's still Indiana," Owen said.

Raymond lifted his beer. "Yeah, but miracles do happen, and there's a new sheriff in town. It seems now Angela has a different cause that will give her the will to get out of bed in the morning."

"And what role did you play in that?"

His dad reached over, rested his hand on his shoulder, and squeezed. "Doing something for my daughter and for you. The way she looks up to you, you did a great job with her."

Owen took in Tessa, who was making her way over

to him, wearing a cream-colored V-neck sweater. Her smile had him thinking he was the luckiest man ever. "She's my sister," he said. "But she always was a handful."

"You're going to make a great father," Raymond added, squeezing his shoulder again before stepping away.

Tessa stepped right up to him, her arms around his waist, and rose up on her tiptoes to offer her lips. He leaned down and kissed her.

"So what am I doing to deserve that?" he said.

"Being almost perfect," she breathed out, staying right where she was. "So, everyone keeps asking when we're getting married."

He slid one arm around her, holding a beer with his other hand. "How about New Year's?"

She pulled back. "I was thinking the summer."

He made a face, leaned down and pulled her closer, and kissed her again. "No, that's too far away. You think I want to give you that much time to freak out, get cold feet, and come up with some reason why the wedding should be called off? No, New Year's, just family, keep it simple. We'll have it here."

She turned serious, not pulling back, then flicked those gorgeous blue eyes back up to him. He could see she was thinking. "New Year's, huh?" She glanced back over her shoulder, and he could see his family watching them with curiosity. When she looked back at him, her smile brightened. "Well, let me think about it…" she teased.

He wrapped both arms around her and kissed her neck. "Seriously, come on."

She laughed that gorgeous quirky laugh she had. "Okay, it's a date."

He leaned in and kissed her. Just then, he heard his mom call out that Christmas dinner was ready, and he felt some crumpled-up wrapping paper hit the side of his head. "Hey!" he said as he pulled back, seeing Luke there.

"Come on, you two," Luke said.

He took in his family, spotting his dad leaning in to kiss his mom.

They were the O'Connells—and for the first time, he felt this tension he'd always carried disappear.

He realized Tessa was still watching him, knowing exactly what he was thinking and feeling.

"He'd do anything for all of you," she said. He knew who she was talking about.

"I know," he breathed out, then leaned down and kissed Tessa again. "Let's go eat."

Turn the page for a sneak peek of
*THE GIRL NEXT DOOR coming next in THE
O'CONNELLS*
Available in print, eBook & Audio

Romance and suspense collide in this haunting romantic thriller.

When special forces operator Luke O'Connell meets a woman he never expected to see again, he uncovers the dangerous secret she is hiding and realizes the lengths someone will go to stop him from uncovering the truth.

Luke never in a million years expected to see Misty Bates again after a weekend of no strings and no names. But when his family introduces him to the nice girl next door, who turns out to be his mysterious fling, he soon figures out that the small-town girl is running from something, and uncovering it could destroy his chance at love.

Luke O'Connell has been unlucky in love because of who he is. He has a job he can't talk about, with trouble always following him, and a peaceful night's sleep is something he can only dream of having.

The O'Connells step in and introduce him to Misty, a nice small-town girl, in the hopes that the two will hit it off, but what they don't know is that Luke and Misty have already met. Years ago, they spent a weekend together after a mission on the other side of the world.

Luke is adamant he's not looking for a relationship, and he can't help seeing red flags behind Misty's nice-girl front. In her, he sees the kinds of ghosts people hide when they're running from something.

Luke doesn't like secrets, and there isn't a secret out there that he can't uncover. He soon discovers that Misty Bates used to be Chloe Welch, and she testified against a local hero after witnessing an unspeakable crime in which a house was burned down and a family perished. But when the small-town jury voted to acquit, the protection she had been promised by local authorities disappeared, and the suddenly hostile residents forced her to leave town.

Luke swears there can never be anything between him and Misty, but his digging has already put her in danger. Two cops show up on her doorstep with an arrest warrant, because the evidence in the case is suddenly pointing in her direction. Someone out there is trying to settle a score, and once again, the O'Connells find themselves deeply embroiled in a scandal, one that could ultimately endanger everyone in the family.

CHAPTER 1

S mall and intimate was how Luke would have described Tessa and Owen's backyard, with its flowers, garden, and privacy. The wedding had been for just close friends and family. He had never seen his brother so happy, and as he leaned on the bar and watched a family he was finding it harder and harder to feel part of, he had to remind himself that his being alone wasn't his brother's fault.

"You're pretty quiet over here, drinking your beer, saying nothing, watching everyone."

He turned to take in Jack, his brother-in-law, who was now the governor of Montana. Four state troopers were present, one at the back gate, another in the yard over by Karen, and two in the small house. He knew that had to be giving the neighbors a lot to talk about. Jack lifted his hand as one of the troopers walked out of the house and over to him, then whispered something.

Jack wore his black suit as if it had been made for him. If Luke had been a girl, he'd have given his brother-in-law a second and third look, too. Jack wasn't as tall as he was, but he thought he might be prettier.

"Just enjoying a beer, Jack," he said.

Jack pulled his gaze, wincing into the sun. By the tug at the corners of his lips, Luke wasn't sure whether he was trying not to laugh or had something else on his mind, likely some humor at his expense. The trooper had walked off and now stood at the back door.

"I see you came alone, no girl on your arm," Jack said. He held a tumbler of bourbon, he thought. His one drink of the night, evidently, or maybe he'd live it up and have two.

Luke didn't even grunt, and he didn't pull his gaze. "Nope." He lifted his beer and downed the rest before putting the bottle on the bar and reaching behind it to pull another from a bucket of ice. He twisted off the cap and heard the sigh from Jack.

"You know everyone feels bad over what happened with Rosemary…"

There it was, that feeling, that sense of discomfort that settled right in the pit of his stomach. No one would let it go, yet he had. He allowed his gaze to settle on Jack with the practiced warning he gave to anyone who risked ending up on his wrong side.

"Is that why you came over, to counsel me about coming solo today?" Luke said. "All my siblings are now married, so should I have dragged some woman along with me? At least then you'd all be happy. Sure, I could have brought a plus one, but there would've been questions, a lot of questions, from my nosy family, and the poor girl doing me a favor would have been running before Owen and Tessa even said 'I do.' I'm not seeing anyone, am not involved, and don't plan on being so anytime soon. Rosemary couldn't have worked, anyway, so you just tell everyone to back off and let themselves off the hook. That was a momentary lapse, thinking someone like me could have something that resembled normal. Being a team guy, I know I can't have a girl waiting at home."

He let the words hang. Did the amusement on Jack's face mean he wasn't buying any of what Luke was saying or something else? That had been the most words Luke had strung together in a conversation with anyone in a long time.

"You know, you can keep telling everyone you're not meant for a relationship, but I know better than anyone that's not true," Jack said. "You should know that your sisters are likely going to take matters into their own hands. Just a heads-up."

He just stared at Jack, who was now leaning on the bar, staring into his tumbler. Something about the way he said it sounded like a warning. He knew something.

"And what matters would those be?"

From across the garden, his sister Suzanne was making a beeline over to them. Her long dirty-blond hair was wavy and styled, and her swelling belly in her gold and white maternity dress meant she was closer to having the baby than not. Harold, her husband of forty-five days, was following her .

"Oh, they figure they need to help you along toward happiness," Jack said. "You know your sisters."

Suzanne slid up beside him, linked her arm in his, and looked at his beer fondly. "You know, being preg-nant, I absolutely miss that ice-cold beer. The taste…"

Luke just lifted a brow and glanced over to Harold. The man had been summoned and was evidently following orders, having reluctantly walked over for a friendly chat. His little sister did have a habit of getting her way.

"Well, you can just live vicariously through me as I enjoy this," Luke said. "So Jack was just giving me a heads-up that you and Karen are up to something, planning on sticking your noses into my life and doing something I'm not going to like. You know my life is my life. Don't be thinking you can fix me or—"

"Jack, you weren't supposed to say anything," Suzanne said. "Anyway, she's a nice girl. You'll like her. And it was Marcus who brought it up, so you can't give me and Karen all the credit. In fact, I think it was Jenny who mentioned it to Ryan first, or was it Tessa?"

His sister looked over to Harold. Now he knew why the man seemed so uncomfortable. He only lifted his gaze in a way that made Luke feel positive he didn't want to answer. "No idea, Suzanne. But Luke is right. You can't be trying to set your brother up. I told you before that this will backfire. Sorry, Luke. I told her. I'm just a bystander." He was holding a beer, his suit jacket gone and his white dress shirt sleeves rolled up.

Luke took in the wedding ring on his sister's finger, remembering the courthouse ceremony, five minutes to say "I do," sign the certificate, and walk out of City Hall. It had been quick, efficient, and nothing like the super romantic backyard celebration of his big brother. He hadn't expected this from Owen, but then, he really was head over heels for Tessa. Apparently, a guy would do anything for the girl he loved.

"I don't need you to find me a girl, Suzanne." Luke lifted his beer and took a swallow, then spotted Karen in a silky red dress that showed off all her curves. He didn't know who she was talking to, but her laughter drifted his way. His mom and dad were across the yard, too, with Alison and Bennett. The rest of the family and a handful of friends had turned this small and intimate event into the kind of party that should have made him happy. And he was happy—for Owen.

Suzanne was still holding his arm. "No, I'm sure you don't, but humor us, okay? Because sometimes we just know better. I think you'll agree when you meet her, and you'll actually thank us for sticking our noses into your life and wanting to fix you up." She fisted her hand and punched his arm playfully in that way of hers, though she really could pack a punch if she wanted to.

Harold lifted his gaze as if he'd already heard this, whereas Jack, he thought, was doing his best not to laugh at his expense. Luke stared down at his sister again, thinking she had too much time on her hands.

"You think you know what I need in my life more than I do? If we're sticking our noses into each other's lives, when is it my turn? I mean, you're due in a few weeks, and then what? Are you staying home to raise the baby? I guess that would be a win-win for Harold, wouldn't it? Kind of every guy's dream, having a bare-foot housewife who'll have dinner ready for him when he gets home, keep his house clean, fetch his slippers, and not talk back."

Suzanne was staring daggers back at him. He knew full well which buttons to push and exactly what to say. Harold said nothing, though alarm flashed in his eyes, and he lifted his hands and stepped back as if wanting to take cover before the sparks flew.

Suzanne hissed, giving him a snarl that wiped her

smile away. "You're such an asshole sometimes," she snapped.

"You know what?" Harold said. "I think I hear Marcus calling me." Apparently, he had been smart enough not to wade into that dangerous territory with Suzanne, and he stepped back farther as if he couldn't believe Luke had brought it up.

Jack still appeared amused and was now shaking his head.

"Don't try spinning this back on me," Suzanne said. "You think I'm not used to how you fight, low and dirty? You toss out fighting words that you know will get under my skin and have me wanting to scratch your eyes out, except you know I'm more likely to slug you… Are you trying to mess with my head? Seriously, Luke, I'm not biting, not today. Tomorrow is a different story, though. Now I'm even more determined to mess with your life.

"And just FYI, after the baby is born, Mom and Charlotte have both said they're willing to step in and help out when I get back to work. And I will, because I've talked to Marcus several times about joining the department. He brushed me off the first three times, saying he can't hire me because I'm family, and Harold and I are married, but I pointed out to him that Charlotte worked there even after he and she were married. There's always the option of being a paramedic, or I could get back my job as a firefighter…"

Luke couldn't believe she'd said that. "The fire department you were fired from is not going to take you back, Suzanne," he said.

Even Jack, who was a master of not showing what he was thinking, seemed surprised. He was now leaning on the bar and hadn't pulled his gaze from Suzanne.

Luke could see his sister was still figuring things out. She'd really loved being a firefighter, but the politics had already decided she had to go.

"Look, I've heard over and over from Harold that there's no chance they'll take me back, but I'm persistent, and there is always a way. Yes, they scapegoated me, but I'm made of stronger stuff, persistence. I'll work the next department over. I've already reached out to the chief, and I still know people there, so I'm not about to take no for an answer. You can stop pushing my buttons with this 1950s 'back to the kitchen' thing. You think I don't know what you're doing, Luke, trying to spin this back on me so I'm not fixing you up? Well, it won't work, because she's already here."

He knew he was frowning, and he realized Jack wasn't surprised. He seemed to already know what was up. A smile had inched its way back into Suzanne's expression as if she was going to make this suddenly painful for him…

"She's here—like, in this backyard, at this wedding?"

Suzanne was really smiling now. She only nodded. Another glance to Jack, and he could see he knew who the girl in question was.

Luke found himself scanning the people, his family, Owen and Tessa's friends, then looked back to Suzanne. "And you…what, want to introduce me and expect some happily ever after? I'll pass."

She tapped his arm and then was somehow pulling him. Damn! For a pregnant woman, she was strong.

"Suzanne, what the hell…?" was all he said, letting his sister lead him across the yard. He spotted Marcus, the best man, dressed in a dark suit, his tie loosened, smiling as if he knew, too. So was Charlotte, wearing a frilly sleeveless blue dress.

"Oh, you just hush up and be nice," Suzanne said.

Ahead of them, Ryan wore a navy suit, standing beside Jenny, with her long dark hair hanging in soft curls. He stepped back to reveal the woman they were talking with, who had short red hair.

"Misty, this is my brother Luke, the one I was telling you about," Suzanne said as they approached.

She looked up, slender, short, wearing a soft green short-sleeved dress that hugged her curves. Luke felt that off feeling he'd had too many times before, taking in those full lips, her oval face, and those eyes, honey gold, a color he'd never forget. Her smile was there one minute, gone the next.

He just stared at her, remembering well the weekend they'd shared together. He felt someone slap his back, one of his brothers, and knew everyone was watching them.

"This is Misty Bates, Tessa and Owen's neighbor and friend," Jenny said.

Luke hadn't looked away. Misty hesitated and then seemed to pull herself together, holding out her delicate small hand. There was that smile again, with those dimples he remembered fondly.

"Hi, Luke. I've heard a lot about you from your family. It's nice to meet you."

So she was playing the game, not wanting anyone to catch on that they had already met. He could call her out or play along. He touched her hand, holding it, and hesitated, feeling the warmth and the unease. Evidently, she wasn't about to come clean.

"Since my family doesn't know how to stay out of

my business, how about we get a drink and exchange numbers?" he said.

He thought it was Marcus who made a rude noise. Luke somehow manoeuvred Misty back to the bar, where Jack was no longer standing, holding out his arm as he walked with her. She wore killer heels, which showed off legs he remembered well.

One, two, three… He had counted their footsteps in his head until they were far enough away from everyone. The tall, lanky bartender was opening a bottle of red wine and glanced at her, saying, "What can I get you?"

"I'll have a glass of that red," she said.

Luke waited for the bartender to pour it. "You know what I remember, Misty, about the last time I saw you?"

She stood so stiffly, lifting her chin as she flicked those eyes at him. He swore he could get lost in them. She said nothing for a moment as she took the glass from the bartender and sipped. "Okay, I'll bite," she replied. "What?"

Luke waited for the bartender to walk away, well aware that everyone in his family was watching them. "One of the best no-strings weekends of my life. But I never expected to see you again. Small world, Misty. Greece is a long way from Livingston."

She only nodded. "It is, at that. So tell me, Luke, when did you join the military? Because I'm pretty sure that when we spent the weekend together, I knew you as a man named Henry who worked for a software company in California, not as Luke O'Connell."

It had been during one of his missions on the other side of the world, when he played the role of someone else. He really hadn't expected to see her again.

"Well, I guess you know I lied. Should I apologize?" He knew he sounded like an asshole.

She lifted a brow. "For lying about who you were or for the no-strings weekend? If I recall, we both agreed. Sure, I could be angry, but instead, let's stand here for a few more minutes and pretend to talk while I drink my wine, and then I'll make my way back over to your family and make my excuses, tell them I'm not interested, that you're not my type or something like that." She was so damn matter of fact.

And she was giving him an out. But there was just something about her, something that seemed different from the woman he had spent that weekend with in Plaka.

"Does that mean you're not up for another no-strings weekend?" he said.

She could have slapped him. Instead, she pulled in a breath and seemed to consider something, lifting her glass to her lips.

Suzanne strode over and slid her hand over Misty's arm before she could answer him. "So are you two hitting it off?" she said.

Of course his sister couldn't leave it alone. The smile was pasted back on Misty's face now, the one that reminded him of a nice girl, but he realized that easy smile was only a front.

She let out a soft laugh. "Luke is great. It was really nice to put a face to the name after all I've heard. But I'm going to make my way back…" She gestured behind her to where Ryan, Jenny, Charlotte, and Marcus were, then lowered her wine and started walking away.

That left him and Suzanne, who was now staring daggers his way again. "What did you say to her, Luke?"

He just took in his sister, then lifted his beer, watching as Misty talked with Jenny and Charlotte. When she looked his way, he realized maybe there was a reason she didn't want anyone to know they'd already met. There was just something about her…

"We just chatted for a minute, Suzanne, until you interrupted," he said.

Suzanne frowned and tapped his arm. "Do you need me to drag you back over there?"

He only shook his head and looked back over to Misty, who was laughing at something Charlotte had said. He knew when a woman was avoiding looking his way. What was it about her? It seemed secrets and lies were just what he attracted.

"Nope," he said. "I already told you I'm not looking for a relationship, Suzanne, and she's not really my type." He hoped she would drop it.

"So what exactly is your type, Luke?"

There it was, the million-dollar question. All he did was lift his beer and take another swallow as he realized Misty Bates was looking right at him.

Billy Jo McCabe Mystery Series

The social worker and the cop, an unlikely couple drawn together on a small, secluded Pacific Northwest island where nothing is as it seems. Protecting the innocent comes at a cost, and what seems to be a sleepy, quiet town is anything but.

The Social Worker

Billy-Jo McCabe wants only to help children overcome their troubled lives, as she herself struggles to forget the childhood nightmare she survived. She took sociology and prelaw at the insistence of her adoptive father, Chase McCabe, and learned how to use power tools from her adoptive mother, Rose. She loves reading in the backs of bookstores before tucking the book back on the shelf and slipping out without paying. She has a fondness for peanut butter and dill pickle sandwiches, has a three-legged cat named Harley, hates running (because that was all she did as a kid), and secretly binges on brownies and red wine on the sofa in front of her TV every Friday night.

She's never been married and has dated only twice. She visits Chase and Rose when summoned and shows up dutifully for every holiday with her family, but she has no siblings to speak of, and she feels a growing resentment for the mother who abandoned her in foster care. Despite proudly maintaining the same prickly attitude that nearly landed her behind bars as a kid, she has yet to speak up to Chase, who interferes in her life too frequently, ready to fix every problem, whether she wants him to or not.

One thing no one knows about Billy Jo is that she moved to Roche Harbor because it's the only clue she has about the last known whereabouts of the woman who abandoned her.

The Cop

Mark Friessen, son of Jed and Diana Friessen, has landed accidently in the role of small-town detective, a position in which he's going nowhere. Nearly married once, and broken-hearted three times, he's sworn he'll stay single forever, and he keeps his tattoo of a former girlfriend as a reminder that only fools fall in love. He's tall, attractive, and stubborn, and he refuses to live in the shadow of his two older brothers, Chris and Danny.

As Roche Harbor's youngest detective, he sleeps with a gun under his pillow. He has a stray dog that won't leave, and he swears that the only two food groups that exist are meat and potatoes. His favorite drink is black coffee in the morning, sugared coffee in the afternoon, and a shot of whiskey in his coffee at night to keep him warm.

From *NY Times* & *USA Today* bestselling author Lorhainne Eckhart comes the first book in the thrilling Billy-Jo McCabe series, which unites two characters from The Friessens and The McCabe Brothers.

Billy-Jo McCabe never expected to become a social worker, considering the broken system nearly destroyed her. Shortly after she takes a job on a remote Pacific Northwest island, she gets a call about an adolescent girl who's gone missing from a wilderness camp, and questions arise about the marks and bruises seen on the young girl's body before she disappeared.

Roche Harbor detective Mark Friessen is called in to investigate the disappearance, but instead of working with the newly appointed social worker, he ends up butting heads and clashing with her every step of the way. Billy-Jo becomes the rival he does his best to avoid, considering the only conversations they have involve her pointing out his shortcomings and arrogance, telling him exactly where he can go.

But when Billy-Jo finds herself in over her head, she's forced to team up with the man she tells herself is her polar opposite, someone she could never be attracted to, as he has the uncanny ability to bring out the worst in her.

The only thing Billy-Jo wants is to find the missing girl and see that she gets the kind of help she herself never got before being tossed in the system—before her father, Chase McCabe, saved her. So, swallowing her pride, she unwillingly forms a truce with Mark, and together, they come up against close-mouthed locals, island secrets that hit too close to home, and the realization that their case about finding and helping a young girl has turned into something far more sinister.

****Each book in this series is a complete book, with no cliff-hangers, and can be read as a standalone. However, these books may contain references to situations from earlier books in the series. As with any long book series that focuses on specific characters, their changing relationships, and how their lives continue to unfold, you may find it more enjoyable to read the series in order of publishing, as there will be developments and changes in the relationship dynamics of the core characters.*

PAYTONPUPPY

Police Chief Mark Friessen and his wife, social worker Billy Jo McCabe, keep a watchful eye on their small island town in the Pacific Northwest. As the couple comes to grips with the fact that a hub of crime run by the political elite has turned the quiet, sleepy Roche Harbor into a playground for the rich and powerful, a young executive of a major international charity moves to town. When Mark and Billy Jo dig deep into the secrets and lies that seem to follow the man, they uncover a twisted truth, one they may wish they had never found.

Newlyweds Mark Friessen and Billy Jo McCabe are back home in the town of Roche Harbor, settling into their life as a married couple while coming to grips with the evil that has woven its web in their small community. Police Chief Mark keeps a watchful eye on all the residents, learning who comes and goes on his island, so when a stranger buys a large property on the west side, Mark shows up on his doorstep to find out why he has moved in.

Walter Crandall tells him the island is home to his five-year-old daughter and his ex-wife, who owns a local bar, and all he wants is to keep a low profile and be left alone to make amends for his mistakes. But there's something about the man that Mark doesn't trust, and when he and Billy Jo begin digging into Walter's past and the charity he was part of, they uncover a deception so twisted they're convinced it can't possibly be true.

The Charity, Chapter 1

Sleeping in was something Billy Jo didn't do, but for the past four days, Mark had opened his eyes to find his wife sound asleep. As he stood in the kitchen, the stove blinking a digital blue 8:10 a.m., he realized he needed to wake her soon.

The coffeemaker beeped, and Mark poured himself a cup of the steaming brew before turning back to the island, on which a file lay open, revealing notes on another thirty of the island's residents. Hesitating only a second, he wondered when he'd become that cop who went digging into civilians' lives, looking for any secrets they might have.

Oh, yeah. When a bunch of criminal elites took up using his island as their personal playground.

He had to roll his shoulders, feeling that punch in the gut again, silently hating the world of people who, at times, were untouchable.

"You didn't wake me."

He turned to see Billy Jo in a blue robe, yawning as

she walked sock-footed past him and pulled a glass from the cupboard to fill with water.

"Figured you needed sleep," he said. "Was going to give you another ten minutes before waking you. You feeling okay?"

She brushed her shoulder-length brown bed hair away from her face and shook her head before drinking down the water. "Fine. Just tossed and turned because of your snoring. What are you doing?"

She settled her glass in the sink, then reached for his coffee and took a swallow of it. As she looked down at the open file, her brow furrowed. He realized she wasn't giving the coffee back, and he couldn't believe she had tossed out that comment about his snoring, considering she had fallen asleep before him.

He leaned down and pressed a kiss to the top of her head, then filled a second mug, a matching green one, from the many wedding gifts that seemed to still be arriving daily from people on the island he'd met only a time or two.

"Looking into the folks who live here," he said, "why they live here, what they do, especially the ones who look too clean. Who lives here full time, part time, and what hidden secrets do they have? You know, the usual investigative thing I do, looking for red flags and skeletons."

Mark filled the mug with coffee and settled the carafe back on the burner. Billy Jo angled her head, glancing over to him in that way of hers. She was complex, with many moods, and he figured something else was coming.

"You were serious, then?" she said, flattening her hand over the file, the notes he'd been reading on

Shirley and Tom Campbell, and pulling it closer to her. "You're really going to investigate every person who lives here and dissect their lives even though they've done nothing wrong? Isn't there some law against that, let alone the fact that you're overstepping a bit?"

She didn't smile and didn't pull that fiery gaze from him. She was the complete package, a woman who was his best friend, his lover, his wife, and she knew how to push every one of his buttons. Damn, he loved everything about her.

He reached for the file in front of her and pulled it away. "Knowing who's on this island and what they're about is something I should have done long ago. You forget what happened here? I don't want that kind of evil ever sneaking in. So yeah, I plan to dissect the lives of everyone who lives here to make sure the members of this community are decent, honest, not looking to set up some criminal enterprise, thinking they can do anything. And that includes our politicians. Consider it my new pastime. I plan to find out everything about them, what they do, who they see, to really dig into their lives. If they are honest people, then they become the people I'm protecting. But how many more criminals are still here, so deep underground that I haven't found them yet? And *yet* is the key word."

She looked up at him, and a smile touched her lips as she leaned against the island, so close to him. "You know all the right things to say sometimes," she said. "Go dig and dissect the lives of anyone and everyone. Oh, and make sure, will you, that you take a second and third look at everyone collecting a check from the DCFS, and especially who rubber-stamped their approvals?"

"They're first on the list—kids and animals." He leaned down and kissed her forehead.

"You're the best," she said. "Damn, I'm going to be late." She lifted the mug and took a swallow. "Oh, and I forgot to tell you we're going to drop in and see Gail tonight. I'll swing by the station after I'm done and we'll head over. I told her we'll bring dinner…"

She had trailed off as she walked back to the bedroom. Then she turned in the doorway, looking back, when he hadn't said anything. The tightness that came every time he thought of Tolly Shephard returned deep in his chest. He knew he'd made a face.

"You have to figure out a way to get past that, Mark," she said. "Gail is our friend."

"Her husband was part of a child trafficking ring."

She let out a heavy sigh. "I know what Tolly Shephard did and didn't do—and what they did to his son to gain his compliance when he played both sides. He's dead, but Gail isn't, and she still has to get up every morning and come to terms with all the secrets Tolly had. Mark, you've turned this island upside down and woken up a lot of people to what has been happening behind their backs. No one saw it. The town council is in a state of flux. You have interim appointees, as the mayor and councilors are now charged, awaiting trial. The entire CPS department has been turned upside down, and jobs are still being vacated. You're a hero for the children, Mark, but you have to know many of the island folks have turned on Gail. Their anger is misdirected. Her truck was spray painted with *CHILD KILLER*. People she's known forever on the island have phoned and said some horrible things…"

"Someone vandalized her truck?" he cut in. "Why didn't she call me? When did this happen?"

Billy Jo glanced over to the window. Her three-legged cat was curled up on the cat tree, whereas Lucky had padded into the kitchen and was lapping water out of his dog bowl. She started back toward him in the fuzzy robe that was more warm than flattering, and he didn't know what to make of the shadows around her eyes. He knew well the places her head went when she struggled. What she was thinking, he had no idea.

"Gail won't phone you," she said. "Not that she thinks you wouldn't show up and file a report, because she knows you would, but I think she believes that because of what Tolly did, she deserves every hateful thing coming at her. Yet every time someone lashes out at her, it kills a little piece of her soul. I can see it. I know Tolly wasn't strong enough to end things the way you did. But I also know he hid it well. So tonight we'll take a pizza over, talk to her and be civilized, and let her know she's a human being and we care."

Maybe it was the way she'd said it, but he wondered whether she understood how he felt about Gail. He couldn't look at her without seeing Tolly.

Instead of saying something, he took another swallow of coffee.

"She thinks you hate her, Mark," Billy Jo said, striding back over to him. She put her mug down on the island, not looking away from what he knew was likely shock staring back at her.

"Excuse me?" he said. "I don't hate her. Where would she ever get an idea like that?"

Billy Jo took another step toward him, sliding her hand on the island to touch the file again, likely seeing the names listed. "Maybe it's because you make excuses never to go and see her. I show up alone, and every time I do, she asks about you, and I feel like I'm cheating when I say you're great but busy, or else you'd be there too. She doesn't believe one word of it, because she can see in my face that I'm lying. Or maybe it's because the last time she saw you was when you told her about Tolly."

Mark pulled his hand over his face, knowing she was right. He could feel the heavy sigh of frustration before it passed his lips.

"You going to make me go alone?" Billy Jo said, pulling her arms over her chest, not looking away.

"I don't hate her," he said. "I just don't know what to say to her. There's a difference."

Billy Jo glanced away, pulling in a deep breath. Then she lifted her gaze, which had softened just a bit. "Sometimes just being there is all that's needed. Don't say anything. Don't pretend. Just pick up a piece of pizza and eat. Can you do that?"

He'd never known Billy Jo to be so reasonable. "I can do that."

She ran her hand over his arm, rose up on her tiptoes, and kissed his cheek. "Good. And you may also want to consider asking Gail to help you dig into the people here. Pick her brain," she said as she reached for her mug and topped it with more coffee.

He wondered if she'd lost her mind. "Breaking bread with Gail is one thing, Billy Jo, but I'm not having her anywhere near this." He knew it had come out rather sharply. He had felt the bite in his words.

Billy Jo blew on the steaming coffee and took a swallow. "Well, that's too bad, because I'm sure she could fill in a lot of holes about a lot of people that you wouldn't otherwise know. And it may help her feel as if she's doing something to make up for what Tolly did. It's a helpless feeling, Mark, feeling responsible even though it's not logical. You could dig and miss something Gail knows that you would never have figured out in a million years. She's been here, like, forever." She tapped his arm again. "Think about it, Mark. That's all I ask."

Then she walked away, and he watched her, her heavy socks, her warm housecoat. This time, she didn't look back.

He reached for the file, seeing the names, as the shower popped on.

"Yeah, there's no way I'm asking Tolly Shephard's widow for help when it comes to anyone on this island," he muttered. Lucky brushed his leg, then looked up at him and whined. "Now, don't go looking at me like that. We'll go see her, eat pizza, and then leave."

There it was again, that sinking feeling he got every time he thought of Gail. As he took in the open file and the notes that only scratched the surface, he couldn't help thinking Billy Jo was too often right. But he wouldn't ask Gail even though she could clear up a lot of questions about a lot of people.

No, involving Gail was exactly what he wasn't going to do.

"Lorhainne Eckhart is one of my go to authors when I want a guaranteed good book. So many twists and turns, but also so much love and such a strong sense of family."

(LORA W., REVIEWER)

New York Times & USA Today bestseller Lorhainne Eckhart is best known for writing Raw Relatable Real Romance where "Morals and family are running themes." As one fan calls her, she is the "Queen of the family saga." (aherman) writing "the ups and downs of what goes on within a family but also with some suspense, angst and of course a bit of romance thrown in for good measure." Follow Lorhainne on Bookbub to receive alerts on New Releases and Sales and join her mailing list at LorhainneEckhart.com for her Monday Blog, all book news, giveaways and FREE reads. With over 120 books, audiobooks, and multiple series published and available at all, retailers now translated into six languages. She is a multiple recipient of the Readers' Favorite Award for Suspense and Romance, and lives in the Pacific Northwest on an island, is the mother of three, her oldest has autism and she is an advocate for never giving up on your dreams.

"Lorhainne Eckhart has this uncanny way of just hitting the spot every time with her books."

(CAROLINE L., REVIEWER)

The O'Connells: *The O'Connells of Livingston, Montana are not your typical family. A riveting collection of stories surrounding the ups and downs of what goes on within a family but also with some suspense, angst and of course a bit of romance thrown in for good measure. "I thought I loved the Friessens, but I absolutely adore the O'Connell's. Each and every book has different genres of stories, but the one thing in common is how she is able to wrap it around the family, which is the heart of each story." (C. Logue)*

The Friessens: *An emotional big family*

romance series, the Friessen family siblings find their relationships tested, lay their hearts on the line, and discover lasting love! "Lorhainne Eckhart is one of my go to authors when I want a guaranteed good book. So many twists and turns, but also so much love and such a strong sense of family." (Lora W., Reviewer)

The Parker Sisters: *The Parker Sisters are a close-knit family, and like any other family they have their ups and downs. Eckhart has crafted another intense family drama… "The character development is outstanding, and the emotional investment is high…" (Aherman, Reviewer)*

The McCabe Brothers: *Join the five McCabe siblings on their journeys to the dark and dangerous side of love! An intense, exhilarating collection of romantic thrillers you won't want to miss. — "Eckhart has a new series that is definitely worth the read. The queen of the family saga started this series with a spin-off of her wildly successful Friessen series." From a Readers' Favorite award—winning author and "queen of the family saga" (Aherman)*

Billy Jo McCabe Mystery: *The social worker and the cop, an unlikely couple drawn together on a small, secluded Pacific Northwest island where nothing is as it*

*seems. Protecting the innocent comes at a
cost, and what seems to be a sleepy, quiet
town is anything but.*

*Lorhainne loves to hear from her readers! You can connect with
me at:*

www.LorhainneEckhart.com
lorhainneeckhart.le@gmail.com

facebook.com/AuthorLorhainneEckhart

twitter.com/LEckhart

instagram.com/lorhainneeckhart

bookbub.com/profile/lorhainne-eckhart

pinterest.com/lorhainneeckhart

In the Silence
In the Charm
Unexpected Consequences
It Was Always You
The First Time I Saw You
Welcome to My Arms
Welcome to Boston
I'll Always Love You
Ground Rules
A Reason to Breathe
You Are My Everything
Anything For You
The Homecoming
Stay Away From My Daughter
The Bad Boy
A Place of Our Own
The Visitor
All About Devon
Long Past Dawn
How to Heal a Heart
Keep Me In Your Heart

The O'Connells
The Neighbor
The Third Call
The Secret Husband
The Quiet Day
The Commitment
The Missing Father
The Hometown Hero
Justice
The Family Secret
The Fallen O'Connell

The Return of the O'Connells
And The She Was Gone
The Stalker
The O'Connell Family Christmas
The Girl Next Door
Broken Promises
The Gatekeeper
The Hunted

The Street Fighter
Finding Home

The McCabe Brothers
Don't Stop Me (Vic)
Don't Catch Me (Chase)
Don't Run From Me (Aaron)
Don't Hide From Me (Luc)
Don't Leave Me (Claudia)
Out of Time

A Billy Jo McCabe Mystery
Nothing As it Seems
Hiding in Plain Sight
The Cold Case
The Trap
Above the Law
The Stranger at the Door
The Children
The Last Stand
The Charity
The Sacrifice

The Wilde Brothers

The One (Joe and Margaret)
The Honeymoon, A Wilde Brothers Short
Friendly Fire (Logan and Julia)
Not Quite Married, A Wilde Brothers Short
A Matter of Trust (Ben and Carrie)
The Reckoning, A Wilde Brothers Christmas
Traded (Jake)
Unforgiven (Samuel)
The Holiday Bride

Married in Montana
His Promise
Love's Promise
A Promise of Forever

The Parker Sisters
Thrill of the Chase
The Dating Game
Play Hard to Get
What We Can't Have
Go Your Own Way
A June Wedding

Kate & Walker
One Night
Edge of Night
Last Night

Walk the Right Road Series
The Choice
Lost and Found
Merkaba
Bounty

Blown Away: The Final Chapter
He Came Back

The Saved Series
Saved
Vanished
Captured

Single Titles
Loving Christine